DATE DUE

Demco No. 62-0549

TRAPPED!

CAGES OF MIND AND BODY

TRAPPED!

CAGES OF MIND AND BODY

EDITED BY

LOIS DUNCAN

Simon & Schuster Books for Young Readers

SIMON & SCHUSTER BOOKS FOR YOUNG READERS
An imprint of Simon & Schuster Children's Publishing Division
1230 Avenue of the Americas, New York, New York 10020

Book design by Symon Chow
The text of this book is set in 11-point Garamond Regular.
Printed and bound in the United States of America
First Edition
10 9 8 7 6 5 4 3
Library of Congress Cataloging-in-Publication Data
Trapped! Cages of mind and body / edited by Lois Duncan.
p. cm.
Summary: A collection of stories by different writers and in various genres in each
of which a young protagonist is trapped in some way, whether emotionally, physically,
or mentally.
ISBN 0-689-81335-X
1. Children's stories, American. [1. Short stories.]
I. Duncan, Lois, 1934–
PZ5.T7317 1998
[Fic]—dc21
97-18049

For my beautiful step-granddaughter,
Sonya Burkin—
may she never be "trapped"
by anything or anybody

CONTENTS

FOREWORD

BY LOIS DUNCAN

The most terrifying reading experience of my life took place in seventh grade when, assigned to "read a short story by an American author," I arbitrarily selected "The Cask of Amontillado." That story conjured up a vision so totally appalling that it became a permanent imprint upon the parchment of my mind. I happen to be claustrophobic, and the mere idea of poor Fortuna—(I knew he was a fictional character, but who cared!)—watching helplessly while a madman sealed him into a crypt, was then, and continues to be, the epitome of horror to me.

Compared to Poe, Stephen King writes like Hans Christian Anderson! Even now, all these many years later, with my own share of life's true horror stories under my belt, I find that story resurfacing in fever dreams in hideous detail, affecting all of my senses—the sight of that last square of light, so quickly obliterated; the sound of a trowel slathering plaster across a brick; then, the dark closing in as the final stone is slowly and deliberately inserted into place. After that, the absolute blackness. The stale scent of motionless air. The piercing eruption of a voice—(Fortuna's or my own?)—as "a succession of loud and shrill screams burst suddenly from the throat of the chained form." And, finally, the chilling realization that, no matter how loudly we scream, there will be no escape.

Fortuna and I are TRAPPED!

So, not surprisingly, when I was offered the challenge of soliciting and editing a collection of short stories by contemporary authors that would leave their mark upon the minds of young adult readers, it didn't take me long to settle upon a theme. I decided to call the anthology *Trapped!* and to offer my writer colleagues free rein to interpret that term in whatever way they chose.

The result turned out to be more than I could possibly have hoped for, an eclectic collection of stories by writers from many different genres that range from adventure to fantasy to humor to romance. Within the following pages readers will meet young protagonists who are trapped—physically, mentally, and emotionally—in situations that draw upon the best and the worst of the human spirit. Alicia lies in the darkness, stroking "the bone basket of her ribs," as she grasps for the strength to free herself from the clutch of anorexia. Calvin, in a desperate attempt to escape from a life of poverty, reluctantly trades one form of entrapment for another. And Hector and Jonathan, trapped by a raging forest fire, discover that manhood demands more than one form of courage.

But there also are stories of fun and frolic and fantasy. The tale of an enchanted princess, held captive in a block of ice as she patiently waits for the lover who is destined to release her. The account of poor, frantic Jill, trapped in a whirlwind of chaos as the only waitress during rush hour at the House of Pancakes. There is even a reinterpretation of the Greek myth about Theseus, trapped in a maze with a Minotaur, "the monster who breathes next to our bed at night," who has been redesigned to symbolize all of life's terrors.

I predict that young readers will find this book difficult to put down. It may even drown out the siren song of the boob tube. Once they take the plunge and dive into the stories on these pages, I believe that they will have the same experience I did when I entered the dark domain of "The Cask of Amontillado."

They will find themselves TRAPPED.

He was imagining how it would feel to be caught there, where you could actually look up through the steep slope of thick underbrush. To hear and see the whoosh of passing traffic: cars, with their roofed skis, moving on, heading to the mountain resorts. Maybe you could see all that life going on up there, going by. You would call out again and again. Help. Help.

The realizing would be slow. For a long time you would still think it was just a matter of getting out. Finding a way out. Then, slowly, the real horror would come. He wondered if you would eventually simply give up, quit calling for help, and wait to die.

A MATTER OF GETTING OUT

BY LOIS LOWRY

On the short ride through the mountains, on the way to the hotel, Gareth's father, rounding a curve, mentioned the accident that had taken place several years before.

"A car went over the edge right there," he said, gesturing to the spot with one hand while steering carefully with the other. "Remember reading about it in the papers?"

"Through the fence?" his mother asked, turning in her seat to peer at the spot as the car continued forward.

"The fence was put up later. There wasn't any fence then, and the car just went over the edge. Apparently it wasn't even going fast. They thought maybe the driver had fallen asleep."

Gareth was only half paying attention. In the backseat, he was trying to read. They were supposed to have finished *Slaughterhouse Five* by Monday, and he was only halfway through. It was hard to concentrate on schoolwork; with graduation coming up, none of it seemed important anymore. But he figured the four days in the mountains would be a good time to finish the book, which he was enjoying.

He expected the time to be boring. It was a legal conference for his father, and Gareth had agreed halfheartedly to come along, to make it a family vacation. His girlfriend had objected, had wanted him to spend the spring break with her, but he had pointed out that it was his last chance to have time with his parents.

"There'll be girls there," Jessie had said, pouting. Gareth had laughed. He was accustomed to coaxing her out of her jealousy.

"No girls," he had reassured her. "Just girl lawyers. All over thirty."

He had tagged along to such things before. There would be events for the nonattorneys, and his mother would complain about the lectures on Italian cooking or contemporary fiction, but she would attend nonetheless and enjoy most of it despite herself.

But for any teenagers there—probably very few, anyway, Gareth knew—there would be little of interest. Outdoor stuff. Hiking. Horseback riding. Gareth hated horses: the smell of them, their unpredictability.

He had only agreed to come with them because he knew he was going to have to tell them. He thought that maybe it would be easier if they weren't at home. At home they'd freak out, big time. But here, at a four-star hotel populated this weekend with lawyers from all over the country, his parents would stay civilized. They'd have to. No scenes.

He kept rehearsing it in his mind. *Dad? Mom?* he would begin. *I want to talk to you about something.*

"Was he killed?" he heard his mother ask. The curve was far behind them now, the place where the accident had happened.

"Well, no, that was the tragic thing. It was February, it went down to below zero for several days, and apparently he froze to death. He hadn't even been badly injured; just a broken shoulder, I think, and a lot of bruises. But he was caught there, in the car. Couldn't get out. And no one reported him missing. His family thought he was off on a ski trip, so they hadn't expected to hear from him."

"Oh, God, just like that movie. With James Caan. What was the name of that?"

"Misery," Gareth told his mother, from the backseat. James Caan should have had a cell phone. He could have just dialed nine-one-one if he'd had a cell phone.

"I saw a TV show once where a guy was buried alive. They thought he was dead, but he wasn't. Luckily he had a cell phone in his casket. And a Bic lighter, so he could see to dial."

"You're kidding," his mother said, looking over the back of her seat at him. His father chuckled.

"It was a pretty stupid show," Gareth acknowledged, and went back to his book.

Now, though, he couldn't concentrate. Now he was imagining how it would feel, to be caught there, where you could actually look up through the steep slope of thick underbrush. To hear and see the whoosh of passing traffic: cars, with their roofed skis, moving on, heading to the mountain resorts; families bickering, maybe the bark of a dog, even the sight of a dog, ears flapped out, nose through a cracked window. Maybe you could see all that life going on up there: going *by*. You would call out again and again. Help. Help.

Night would be the worst. No traffic up here at night. So even the hope would be gone, then, and you would feel the hunger and cold. You would replay it in your mind: the trip, the false move, maybe falling asleep, maybe simply being distracted, looking elsewhere, not noticing the curve, making a wrong choice, all of it happening too fast. The dizzy spin downward; the coming to rest; being alive, still, not even terribly injured; maybe even laughing aloud at the surprise of thinking yourself lucky; thinking it could be undone. Then, trying to extricate yourself, and realizing you were caught.

The realizing would be slow. For a long time you would still think it was just a matter of getting out. Finding a way out. Then, slowly, the real horror would come. He wondered if you would eventually simply give up, quit calling for help, and wait to die.

Gareth went back to his book, willing himself to read the chapters, though the image still lingered, along with his awareness of the difficult conversation still ahead.

Dad? Mom? Listen, I know you're not going to like this, but I've decided—

Actually, Jessie and I have decided—

Distracted, he shifted in his seat and turned an unread page.

"A suite! Cool," Gareth said, looking around. Entering the smaller bedroom, he set his bag on the bed, checked the folded cardboard on top of the TV to see what movies were available (He'd seen all four. Bummer.), and looked through the window at the golf course below. Men in pastel trousers were comparing clubs and waiting for their turn at the tee. Middle-aged jerks. That's what Jessie called them, her voice sarcastic, her deep blue eyes sparkling with contempt.

"Gar?" His dad was there, in the bedroom door. Not a jerk at all. He was wearing jeans. His greying hair was unruly—as usual, he needed a haircut, but he said he never had time—and was unwrapping one more of the endless sticks of gum he chewed to get him through not smoking.

"Six weeks?" Gareth asked.

His father grinned, folded the stick of Doublemint, and popped it into his mouth. "Six weeks, two days, and four hours. But who's counting?"

"You're addicted to gum, now." But he was proud of his father.

"You want to go down to lunch with us? Mom's unpacking, but she'll be ready in a minute."

"Sure."

Maybe at lunch he could bring it up. *Listen, guys, I've been giving it a lot of thought, and I've decided against college.*

No, ah, not just postponing. The thing is, Jessie and I have decided to get married. So I'm going to get a job. They're looking for management trainees at Wal-Mart.

Oh, God. The looks on their faces. He remembered how they'd looked when he was notified of his early acceptance at Princeton: the excitement, the pride. They'd never understand this. Why he didn't want Princeton or the rest of it. How he could portray it to them so that they could see what he and Jessie saw: the contentment of a little apartment somewhere, nothing fancy, and being together at the end of the day, coming home from their jobs, cooking together, watching TV, no demands. None of the frustrations that his own parents had: the mortgage, the office stuff, preparing for trials, meetings, committees, his mom's volunteer work, all of it so upwardly mobile, so middle-class, so stereotyped; what was it Jessie said—

We don't want the rat race.

They would think Jessie was pregnant.

"Ready? I'm starving." His mother was there, wearing a plaid blouse, her hair pulled back in a ponytail. She looked like Michelle Pfeiffer, older. In his baby pictures, holding him, she was beautiful. She—they—had wanted other children, but it hadn't happened.

Jessie wanted two. A boy and a girl; it would be okay if they were twins. But not right away. Maybe after they had saved a little money. But she had chosen names already. Cute names. Gareth couldn't remember what they were.

He wondered if the man in the car had had a wife and children.

No, of course she isn't pregnant. And she has a pretty good job lined up, at a bank. She starts right after graduation. We'll get married first, though. She wants to go to Hawaii for a honeymoon. Her friend went to Hawaii, and the hotel had a swimming pool with a bar that you could swim right up to—

No, that would be dumb to mention a bar. Jessie was only seventeen, and he was eighteen. They wouldn't get carded at a Hawaii hotel if they were in a pool and on a honeymoon, but still, it would not be wise to bring up the bar to his parents. It would be a distraction from the main issues.

The vast dining room was mirrored, so that the view from the huge west wall of windows was reflected and they seemed to be surrounded by sky, mountains, and the lavish hotel gardens bright with early spring flowers. The tablecloths were pale blue, and the waitresses, in pale blue dresses, moved among the crowd of guests, distributing menus and smiles. Gareth gave his order for a club sand-wich to a pretty dark-haired girl whose name tag said AMY.

Maybe this isn't the greatest time to talk about this, but—

Their food arrived. His sandwich was held together with toothpicks wearing pale blue paper frills. Gareth looked at it, startled, and heard the waitress giggle. She shrugged her shoulders and rolled her eyes.

"She's cute," his mother said, smiling, as the waitress went away. "Awfully young."

Mom, Dad—

"Keith!" A handsome man in tennis clothes stopped beside their table and greeted Gareth's father. "Good to see you! And this is your family?"

His dad introduced them to the man, an old friend from Seattle, a classmate of his father's from law school. "My wife, Betsy. And this is my son, Gareth."

"Your boy looks like you, Keith. Going to be a lawyer like your dad, Gareth?"

Gareth smiled politely. "No, sir, I don't think so."

"Gar's going to Princeton in the fall. He's planning to major in English, The world has enough lawyers, don't you think, Steve?" Both men laughed.

They exchanged pleasantries and plans for the day, and eventually the man drifted away. Now his mother was talking about tennis; she pointed out the courts to him, barely visible beyond the gardens. Around them was a clink of forks against plates, the murmur of conversation and soft laughter; the pale blue dresses of the waitresses moved in a pattern through the dining room, emerging from the door to the kitchen with laden trays, threading their way smoothly through the tables, returning to the kitchen again. The girl named Amy took Gareth's empty plate away and brought him a piece of pie.

His parents talked, laughed, smiled. It was not the right time. Tonight, perhaps.

After lunch, Gareth changed to shorts and took his tennis racket over to where he had seen the courts. He made his way down a flagstone path through the gardens. There were no sounds from the courts; usually, he thought, you would hear the thump of balls and the laughter and shouts of players. Maybe it was too soon after lunch. But there might be someone waiting for a partner, someone who could volley some with him; or he could simply hit a few balls against the backboard.

The sky, cloudless, was a vast blue expanse, and he saw a hawk soar effortlessly beyond the trees, its wings stationary in the current of the air.

He approached the small clubhouse beside the courts and glimpsed, suddenly, the same pale blue that had dotted the dining room. Then he heard a voice, and saw that the waitress, the one with AMY printed on her plastic name tag, was leaning against the clubhouse wall, the receiver from a pay phone against her ear. Her voice as she took their order had been cheerful and outgoing; now she sounded upset.

Not wanting to interrupt or intrude, Gareth stopped and waited beside a large evergreen.

"I *can't*," he heard the waitress named Amy say in a frustrated voice. "I'm already in trouble because you called during lunch and said it was an emergency. A couple of tables complained because they had to wait."

He could see her frown, listening to whomever was on the other end. "Look," she said in exasperation, "I have to start setting up at four, and if I leave here now and drive down, I'll never get back in time. It's already two o'clock. If I don't show up at four I'll lose my job. What about your mother? Why don't you call her?"

He waited. Odd, how he hoped she could work out whatever was a problem for her. She was nothing to him. They had nothing in common, except their age. She looked about eighteen.

He heard her start to cry. "Well, tell her she has to!

"Or else *you* do it!" she said angrily. "So what if you lose your job? It's not like it would be the first time!"

She slammed down the receiver and stood there crying. Then she turned and saw him.

"I'm sorry," Gareth said. "I didn't mean to eavesdrop, but I just walked up and I couldn't help overhearing."

She took a deep breath, wiped her eyes with the back of her hand, and said defensively, "We're allowed to use this phone."

"Well, sure," he said awkwardly, "no problem. I didn't even mean—"

He saw a drink machine. "You want a Coke or something?"

"My baby has a fever, and the day care says we have to come take her home."

"You don't have to explain. I mean, I'm sorry about the baby. I hope she's okay."

She sighed. "Yeah, she's okay. She's teething. They get fevers sometimes when they're getting teeth. But the day care can't keep them if they have a fever. It's a state law."

Gareth found change in his pocket and extricated two drinks from the machine. He handed the waitress one.

"What's her name?" he asked. Since he couldn't solve her problem, he resorted to small talk and pleasantries.

"Ashley."

It sounded familiar. He remembered that it was the name that Jessie had already chosen for their future baby girl. The boy, he remembered suddenly, was to be Tyler. Or maybe it was Schuyler.

"Do you have any other kids?"

She stared at him. She had seemed so young, so pretty, at lunch, grinning at him mischievously about the silly frilled toothpicks. Now, with her hair uncombed and her face blotched from crying, she looked harder, less attractive.

"Other kids?" she asked with a harsh laugh. "What're you, out of your mind?"

She sat beside him on the bench beside the tennis court fence, the bench where players would sit to change their shoes. He glanced down at his own sneakers, and then at her feet. She followed his eyes, looked at the sensible white lace-up shoes that all waitresses wore, and tucked her feet under the bench.

He had not noticed her wedding ring at lunch. Now he did.

More small talk. "What does your husband do?" he asked politely.

"When he works, you mean?" Her voice was resigned. Right now he loads trucks for a van line. He'd like to get to be a driver."

Ah, thought Gareth: upwardly mobile.

The waitress rose, tossed her empty soda into the trash can, and picked up her purse, which she had left by the pay phone. "Here," she said, opening her purse.

"Oh, that's okay. My treat," Gareth said quickly. "You don't need to pay for it."

"No, I meant: Here; I wanted to show you this. It's Ashley."

She thrust an opened wallet at him, and he glanced at a photograph of a plump baby dressed in pink, staring with a confused look at the camera.

"Cute," Gareth lied, and handed it back. The waitress

nodded, returned the wallet to her purse, and turned to leave. "Guess I'll see you at dinner," she said. "The special's salmon tonight."

"Yeah, okay, see you."

He whacked tennis balls against the backboard until some strangers showed up, needed a fourth for doubles, and asked him to play.

Much later, back at the hotel, closing the glass door behind him as he entered the shower, Gareth had an odd thought.

What if the latch on the shower door broke as you closed it? What if it became inoperable? And you couldn't open it from the inside?

There you'd be, taking your shower, enjoying the rush of hot water on your sweaty body, scrubbing shampoo into your hair, maybe even singing some stupid song—his father always did that in the shower, sang old Cole Porter songs—and then you rinsed off the shampoo and soap, turned the water off, and tried to open the door. *But it wouldn't open.*

Gareth chuckled at the thought and examined the glass and tile walls around him, wondering if he could possibly climb them and escape. But it looked impossible.

Could you break the glass door somehow? Probably not without severing an artery and bleeding to death, he thought.

You'd just have to yell for help. Eventually someone would come. The maid, to turn down the bed. It would be embarrassing, having the maid find you, but it would beat starving to death in a little tiled cell.

It was not like the guy in the car, for whom no one came.

Casually, still rubbing shampoo into his hair with one hand, he reached down and tested the door. The latch moved efficiently and it opened.

Laughing self-consciously, he closed it again and continued his shower.

The waitress named Amy was not at dinner. Perhaps, Gareth thought, they assigned them different areas. He looked around the huge dining room but didn't see her anywhere.

He ordered the special from a middle-aged waitress named Claire and asked her, when she brought his salmon, what had happened to Amy.

The waitress didn't know. "I don't even know which one she is," she told Gareth. "They come and go. Maybe she didn't show up tonight. Half the time they don't show up, the young ones. They find something better to do.

"Enjoy," she said, meaning their three plates of salmon, and turned to a nearby table with her order pad ready.

His mother was curious, he could tell from her look.

"I saw her after lunch at the tennis court," he explained, "and we talked for a while."

"I didn't realize they let the employees play tennis."

"She wasn't playing," Gareth explained. "She was just making a phone call. They let them use the phone out there."

"She was very attractive."

Gareth nodded noncommittally.

In the lobby after dinner, Gareth saw the man named Steve who was his father's friend.

"Here's Keith's boy!" the man said in a loud voice. He turned to introduce Gareth to his wife. "He's going to Yale next fall!"

Gareth corrected him. "Princeton," he said.

Walking back to the room, he began to rehearse a conversation in his mind. Not on the phone. It would be when he got back. It would be in person. It would not be easy.

Jessie? Listen. We have to talk.

A NOTE FROM LOIS LOWRY

When I was twenty-five years old, in November of 1962, I got up early one morning—a little before six—to put the Thanksgiving turkey into the oven. Then I sat down in a rocking chair that I kept in the kitchen, and fed my new baby, three-week-old Ben.

It was a pleasant, comfortable scene. The kitchen had warmed up because of the oven, and was beginning to smell Thanksgiving-ish. Ben was a good baby, undemanding and sweet-smelling as he nursed. I rocked, and thought about the writing course I was taking, and how I had gotten behind in the assignments but thought I might catch up over the Thanksgiving weekend.

After a few minutes, I could hear the padding sound of little pajama-clad feet coming down the hall of the apartment. My three-year-old son, Grey, his sleepers stained from spilled liquid antibiotics—Grey seemed to have a perpetual ear infection that year—appeared in the kitchen and announced that he needed Cheerios immediately.

Then his sister, Alix, four years old, appeared beside him. "Kristin's awake," she announced sleepily. "She wants to get out of her crib. And her diapers smell bad."

So I put the new baby into his bassinet, poured Cheerios for the two toddlers, went to change the thirteen-month-old, and decided that I would never catch up on the assignments, would never complete the course, would never get my college degree, would never become a writer; probably the turkey gravy would be lumpy as well, and I should just resign myself to a lifetime sentence of uncomplicated aspirations.

But somehow I put it all together. It took a long time and it wasn't easy. I got the degree, wrote the books—twenty-four of them so far—and the little girl who was four that Thanksgiving will be thirty-nine the next time it rolls around.

If my parents, when I announced to them at age eighteen that I was dropping out of college to get married, had raised objections (They didn't. That amazes me now.), I wouldn't have listened. I wonder, though, if I had read—and I was a voracious reader—a story of early marriage that had included the soggy Cheerios and lumpy gravy, the midnight howling of toddlers with ear infections, the smelly diapers, the dawn demands, and the deferred dreams, would it have made a difference?

Probably not. But there is always that chance.

Still holding on to his hair, I stand and pull him up with me. He seems like he's calmed down some. I'm not sure what I should do with him now. I see all the women's faces at the kitchen window. I'm about to yell for one of them to drive down to the Sac-N-Pac to use the pay phone and call the police when Watkins spins away from me, leaving me with a handful of dirty blond hair. He's diggin' into his front pocket and he's got this mean little smirk on his face. That's when I remember the knife.

SHEEP

by Rob Thomas

arlette tells me to check the locks—again.

So I do. But it's kinda pointless. I never been in a house this safe. All the windows have bars on 'em. The doors have three dead bolts. There's even a little camera that shows you who's at the front entryway. Or there used to be anyway, until about twenty minutes ago when Mrs. Watkins's drunk husband took a Louisville Slugger to it. Ain't nothin' but fuzz on the monitor now. Not that we really need it; we know he's still out there. We can hear him.

"Woman! Get out here, woman! Worthless piece of . . ."

He'll stop for a few seconds to take another swig from his bottle. Then start up again.

Carlette picks up the phone one more time. It's still dead. Naturally. Did she think he was gonna feel bad and repair the box once he smashed it up? She walks back over to where Estella and Patrice are holding Mrs. Watkins's hands and trying to make her relax. Carlette pats her on the back.

"He can't get in. You'll sleep here tonight. We can deal with him when he sobers up or have him arrested if you like."

Mrs. Watkins doesn't say anything. She just sits there and shakes.

I turn and stare out the window and watch her husband. I just don't understand people sometimes. How'd she ever end up with this Billy Ray Cyrus-haircut-stealing, number 76 mesh shirt-wearing, beer-gutted, no butt-having, sweaty, gutter-mouthed piece of cracker trash anyway? I glance back at Mrs. Watkins, her makeup smeared all over her face.

Okay, so maybe I understand the match.

"Shawn?" says Carlette.

"Uh-huh?"

"Could you check the doors again?"

I don't argue. I just do it.

They've never really liked me here. I don't think they really like anyone with a Y chromosome though, so I try not to let it stress me out. You can't really blame 'em. The Deerfield Home for Battered Women deals with a lot of loser men. They just take it out on the rest of us. They used to never let men within the walls, but after the "incident," they decided they'd better have someone out here just in case. No one will give me the whole story, but from what I've heard, it was pretty bad. Some boyfriend got so mad after they convinced his main squeeze/punching bag to leave him that he came out looking for her. When he didn't find her, he took it out on whoever was working. I don't know who it was—they won't tell us—but I don't think he just beat her up. It sounds like the bars and locks and the monitor have all been added since then too.

They couldn't afford to hire a real security guard, so they talked to Coach Rossy, and he got a few of us—his offensive line mainly, I'm the only basketball player—to come up here just so they have a male around for emergencies. Which is what this is, but I still don't feel very useful. He ain't getting in this fortress. I can tell you that. But on the other hand, we ain't goin' nowhere either.

The Home is set on six acres way the hell out here in the country, and ain't nobody supposed to know where it is, 'cept the ladies they bring out here. They make all the volunteer muscle sign a little contract sayin' we won't tell a soul, but who could we tell that would care? I'll give odds right now, Mrs. Watkins spilled it. Maybe she left the address lying out on a scrap piece of paper "accidentally." Maybe she "let it slip" to a sister-in-law. But it's me who's getting the dirty looks every time her old man screams that he's gonna beat her like a dog.

Patrice dampens a washcloth with warm water and uses it to wipe away Mrs. Watkins's tears. The woman's makeup comes off at the same time, and you can see the bruises around her eyes. It makes me think of my sixth birthday, which I've kept out my mind for years.

I need a weapon.

Finding one isn't that hard. The Home has a fireplace where all the ladies like to sit around, sip coffee, and pretend everything's chill. I pick up one of the tools sitting out next to it, not the brush or shovel, the good one—the poker. I give it a couple practice swings.

"Shawn!"

Carlette's shooting icicles at me.

" 'Sup?"

"Come with me," she says, moving toward one of the back bedrooms.

I set down the poker and follow her. She waits until she can close the door behind me to start yelling.

"Do you want to upset Mrs. Watkins even more than she already is?"

"Upset her? I want to go take care of the guy who's callin' her names," I say. "It's time *someone* stood up to him."

If she was ticked when she first got in the room, now Carlette's about ready to explode. Sort of makes me wish I'd kept hold of the poker. At first she can hardly speak, she's so mad. She gets started a couple of times.

"You . . ."

She shakes her head and clenches her fists.

"You . . ."

She bites her lip and stares at the ceiling.

Carlette ain't pretty to begin with, but gettin' all

excited, she's downright scary lookin'. I'm thinkin' this when she finally gets the words out of her mouth.

"You ignorant little boy."

She's crossin' a double yellow line with that one.

"Watch it, lady. You don't pay me nothin'."

"You have no idea what standing up really means. You don't have a clue what that poor woman has gone through."

"I know that if I was her, I'd've been long gone by now."

For a second I think Carlette might slap me, but she knows better.

"You arrogant—"

"You better back off."

Carlette takes a deep breath.

"Let me tell you a story," she says. "Then you can tell me how you'd handle things if you were her."

"Whatever."

"All right." Carlette sits down in a rolling desk chair that's handy. "There aren't a lot of choices available to Mrs. Watkins. Now I can't tell you why she ever fell in love with that piece of work outside, but she did, and she has three kids to show for it—two girls and a boy. She had the first when she was fifteen. She hasn't been back to school since. Do you know what kind of job a ninth grade education qualifies you for? Do you know how much money it takes to feed and clothe and put a roof over the heads of three children?"

"Why doesn't she just divorce him and get on welfare? Or press charges when he hits her."

"That easy, huh?"

"Just tell me."

Carlette drums her fingers on the desk before speaking again.

"Partially for her kids. He's an electrician, makes good money. Treats the kids all right. He never hits her in front of them. But they're getting older. One of her daughters has started asking about the bruises. Plus, she figures he's the best she can do."

"What?"

"She's got three kids. She's poor. She's uneducated. Her looks are gone. I try to tell her she's not even thirty."

"I would've guessed forty."

"They haven't been easy years."

"I still don't get what you think is so brave about her."

"Well, she's here. She's trying to get out. She's risking everything—more beatings, losing the only man who may ever love her. Children, when they don't understand why parents break up, tend to blame the one who leaves or forces the split. Her children could actually choose their dad over her. Now, Shawn, do you think you could risk all that?"

But I'm not really listening to Carlette anymore. I'm six years old again.

I've got a mouth full of cake. It's late at night. I remember looking at those presents all day, asking Mama, "Can I open one now? Now? Huh? Just one?"

And Mama sayin', "When your daddy gets home. He wants to be here."

So we wait . . . and wait . . . and wait. Through Cosby, *through* Hill Street Blues, *through the news.*

"Can I open one now?"

"You can open them all," she says.

She lights the candles on my cake and tells me to wish for earplugs.

I finish tearing the wrapping paper off a Tony Dorsett autographed pair of cleats when Daddy comes through the door. I remember being juiced about showing him what all I'd gotten. He comes over and picks me up by an arm and leg and spins me around the room like an airplane, and I can't stop gigglin' and carrying on. Finally, just when I start thinkin' I'll throw up from dizziness and laughing so hard, he puts me down and hugs me. The he pulls a Snickers outta his pocket and hands it to me. Standin' so close to him, I remember thinkin' how funny he smells, like flowers. Not like a daddy.

I fall asleep that night holding on to my new stuffed dog. I'd been beggin' for a real one, but the apartments didn't allow pets. The first thing I think when I wake up is that the building must be on fire. Mama is screaming, and I can hear stuff bouncin' against the wall that separates my room from theirs. But no one comes to get me. For a while I lay awake thinking

I will burn alive. I must be trying hard not to hear what they're saying.

"You ruined my life! You ruined my life!"

Mr. Watkins's yelling causes Carlette to drop her stare. Someone knocks on the door she closed behind us. Carlette says come in. Patrice cracks open the door.

"I think you better see this," she says.

Whatever "this" is, it's got Patrice pretty agged. I follow Carlette out into the kitchen, where we have the best view of the grounds. I hear glass breaking before I make it to the window. I'm thinking it would be best to get the ladies into the garage, where there aren't any windows, Mr. Watkins couldn't get in through the burglar bar if he wanted, but once I can see what's going on, I realize that precaution won't be necessary. He isn't trying to get in the house.

Out in the circular driveway, the staggering wife-beater is demolishing Carlette's Corolla. He smashes the last window and starts pounding on the hood. Then he takes out a good-sized pocketknife and slashes the two front tires. He's stopped calling his wife names; he's moved on to the women working in the shelter. He gets pretty ugly. He makes it pretty clear that he doesn't consider them *real* women.

I look to Carlette for a sign. She still looks mad, but not any more mad than she's been since the redneck got here. Mrs. Watkins has started back up crying. She keeps sayin' "I'm sorry" over and over again. Patrice and Stella are hardly payin' any attention to Mr. Watkins anymore, they're too busy trying to calm down his wife. I think Estella ought to show a little interest since it's her car parked next to Carlette's. My eighty-nine Grand-Prix is third in the row. I got it used for six hundred dollars from Delvoe Ford after I signed with UT. Great deal, but then he's alumni. He's supposed to give me a break.

I can't believe we're all just standing here watching him. Doing nothing. Like sheep. He stands up on the trunk of Carlette's car and starts unzipping his fly.

"Come and get it," he shouts. "You know you want it."

Then he starts whizzin' through the broken window into Carlette's backseat. I'm down to the final lock on the back door, the sliding bolt, before Carlette notices I'm no longer standing next to her. I hear her shout my name, but it's too late. I'm out.

I'm not really thinking. I'm just sprinting around the house in the direction that'll make me come up behind him. As I turn the last corner, I see him. He's up on the trunk twirling the baseball bat around in his hand and laughing. I don't even slow down. I take two more steps, then jump. My shoulder hits him just below the knee, and I can feel him give out and start to fall. The trouble is, hitting him didn't slow me down enough, so I go fly-ing all the way into the car. I scramble up in time to see him crawling along the ground behind the car, reaching for the bat. As he's crawling away from me, I can see a blood stain growing on his jeans. The whiskey bottle he kept in his back pocket must have shattered when I flipped him. Good. He gets hold of the bat before I can catch up to him, but I'm on top of him so fast that he can't swing it. I push him down onto his stomach and force his head sideways into the dirt. He's sort of panting. I yank back on the man's scraggly hair and tell him to let go of the bat. There's nothing he can do with it anyway, all sprawled out like this. His fingers release it. Still holding on to his hair, I stand and pull him up with me. He seems like he's calmed down some. I'm not sure what I should do with him now. I see all the women's faces in the kitchen window. I'm about to yell for one of them to drive down to the Sac-N-Pac to use the pay phone and call the police when Watkins spins away from me, leaving me with a handful of dirty blond hair. He's diggin' into his front pocket and he's got this mean little smirk on his face. That's when I remember the knife.

"She's doin' you too?" he says.

Before he can get his hand out of his pocket, I pick up the bat and break his arm with it. I can hear it snap. But the peckerwood is too drunk and too mad to just hang it up. He charges at me, but I sidestep him, stick out my foot, and watch him fly. I get on top of him, knees on his shoulders right away. We're in the lawn right in front of the kitchen window. I start shouting at the women inside.

"Go use the pay phone at . . ."

That's when Watkins spits at me, and takes over shouting at the window.

"You're worthless. You're nothing."

I try wrapping my pillow around my head. It doesn't help.

I smash Watkins in the mouth and tell him to shut up.

Daddy's not at breakfast the next morning. Mama's wearing sunglasses.

I punch him again. His teeth cut my knuckles.

I'm yelling at Mama, "What'd you do? Why'd you make him go away?"

I spit back in his face, but I'm not sure he's conscious.

It's my ninth birthday. Mama's married to someone else. I'm blowing out candles at Gramma's.

The knife is sticking out of Watkins's pocket. I reach down and pull it out.

"Shawn!"

I see Daddy again the day I sign to play for the Longhorns. He gets on TV sayin', "That's my boy."

I pull out the blade.

"Shawn! No!"

I look up. Carlette's running across the lawn with Mrs. Watkins right behind her. Carlette slows down when she gets up to me.

"Hand me the knife, Shawn."

Watkins makes some sort of groaning sound. His face is bloodied up pretty good, but he's breathing. I fold up the blade and hand it to Carlette. As I'm giving up the knife,

Mrs. Watkins slaps me and drags her fake fingernails across my face.

"Get off him," she sobs.

"You crazy—"

"Shawn, come here." Carlette's talkin' to me in that same mad-as-hell tone she used to call me into the bedroom. I'm about tired of her, but I pick up the bat and follow her to a spot by the front door that's swinging open.

"I want you to see what you've done," she says.

She motions with her head back toward where Watkins is laid out. Mrs. Watkins is cradling her husband's head in her hand, snifflin' away.

"I'm sorry, baby," she says. She tries to wipe blood away with his shirt. "I'm so sorry. I never shoulda come out here. I'm so, so sorry. I can't believe what they done to you. I'm so sorry. It'll be all right."

"Happy?" says Carlette.

I think about it for a few seconds.

"Sort of," I say.

She takes another look back at Mrs. Watkins.

"I guess you can be, Shawn," she says. "*You're* free to go."

A NOTE FROM ROB THOMAS

When I was twenty, my roommate's girlfriend volunteered at a shelter for battered women. My sense of what goes on inside owes largely to stories she'd tell—always leaving out the names—of the kind of abuse these women experienced.

Though the address of that shelter where she worked was a secret, the founders had taken the additional precaution of selecting a house fifty yards from the highway patrol office. (My roommate and I provided occasional transportation; because of that, we were two of the only men in town to know the location.)

A decade later, when asked to come up with a story with a "trapped" theme, I thought again of that house. What if one of those violent husbands or boyfriends knew the shelter's location? What if it wasn't a stone's throw from the police station? What if there was no way out and no way to call for help?

Under this premise, I was able to "trap" my protagonist, but during the writing of "Sheep," I became less interested in the physical sense of the word and more intrigued by the larger issues that create a need for these institutions.

"Sheep" is one of twelve stories I wrote about teenagers completing community service projects in order to graduate from high school. Ten of these stories are compiled in my own collection, *Doing Time:*

Notes from the Undergrad, and another, "The War Chest" was included in the compilation *Twelve Shots: Outstanding Short Stories about Guns*, edited by Harry Mazer. My novels include *Satellite Down*, *Slave Day*, and *Rats Saw God*.

That morning the psychiatrist had asked, "Why are you starving yourself?" and she had known all the right answers. Escaping the responsibilities of growing up, having control over something at least, being beautiful, perfect, for once, making people pay attention, love her. She smiled to herself that she could know all this and still skip dinner, still jog five miles in the rain.

She had not told the psychiatrist about Peter.

THE BOX

BY Francesca Lia Block

Alicia lay on the bed in the dark, touching the bone basket of her ribs, the bone bird of her hipbones. Although she was wrapped in blankets, she felt cold. The room she shared with Peter was really a sunporch. All summer they had looked out at the plum tree and honeysuckle and felt the sun through the glass. But now it was autumn and raining. The tree in the yard was a skeleton like the one Alicia's father used to use in his anatomy class.

Alicia's stomach made noises like a cat as she curled up under the blankets. She did not shut her eyes. She did not want to see what was there in her head—the naked body, all bones and whiteness, crouched in a marble box. But she could not escape the voice that easily.

I will not eat cakes or cookies or food. I will be thin thin pure. I will be pure and empty.

That morning the psychiatrist had asked, "Why are you starving yourself?" and she had known all the right answers. Escaping the responsibilities of growing up, having control over something at least, being beautiful, perfect, for once, making people pay attention, love her. She smiled to herself that she could know all this and still skip dinner, still jog five miles in the rain. She had not told the psychiatrist about Peter.

During her first months away from home, she had wandered on the campus looking into the faces of the men. Then, at a party, she had seen Peter wearing a white shirt and drinking gin. He looked like the pictures of her father when he had first met her mom—long legs, narrow chest, a shyness of eyelashes.

He walked her to the dorm, and the air smelled rich and sooty after the rain, like flowers could grow in it.

"You look like a poet," she said when he told her what was in the notebook with the torn binding.

"It frustrates me. It's all just this pretentious self-centered angst. I want it to change things."

When he kissed her good night and held her for a moment, she was surprised at how cool his skin felt, except for the heat in the hollow of his back. The memory of that heat through his thin shirt stayed in her palms all night. When she touched herself in her dorm bed, she said his name out loud in the dark. She wanted to tell him that he had already changed something.

A few nights later, they went to a café in the city with sawdust floors and steamy windows. Peter talked about the Beats who used to hang there, reciting their poetry.

A skinhead with a swastika tattoo walked by the window, screaming, "Kill the Jews!"

Alicia's knuckles whitened around the edge of the table.

"I don't think violence is ever justified," Peter said, pouring Alicia more bright gold white wine from the glass decanter.

She wanted to make the swastika bleed. But to Peter she just said, "Never?"

He must have heard the tightness of her voice. He looked out across Broadway at the nipples of a neon sex goddess flashing on and off. "I know. I know. Maybe," he said.

He bit his lip. It was full and soft in contrast to his narrow face. Alicia felt her thighs weaken, like the muscles were sponges soaking up wine.

That night in his tiny dorm bed, the heat she had discovered in Peter's back pulsed through her whole body. She looked into his eyes and saw herself trapped in the irises.

After that, they were inseparable, always holding hands, always touching, almost bound together. Like two bodies wrapped up as one mummy, Alicia thought. They felt as if nothing else, no one else mattered. Most weekends they would take BART to the café and pretend to be different people.

"What do you think of the way Vermeer used light?" she asked him. She was playing the older-woman artist.

The woman with the bay-windowed house full of flowering cactus plants that you had to water very gently by pouring drops just into the center of the spiny green leaves. The frankincense-and-myrrh-scented woman with the huge hoop earrings and turquoise rings, and lines carved around her eyes.

"You'll have to take me to some museums," he said. He was being the young man on the road, following the sun because gray weather made him suicidal, writing his poetry on the walls of gas station men's rooms across the country. "But I did see a show of—I think his name was Hopper— once. And I like his light. It was kind of lonely or something."

Or, "'The world's a mess, it's in my kiss,' like John and Exene said," he mumbled. They were being punks on acid with skunk-striped hair and steel-toed boots.

"Fuck, yes. Let's go to Mexico, shave our heads, get drugs, wear beads and silver."

Once, he pretended to be a professor teaching her about William Carlos Williams. He came up behind her, so quiet, while she was reading, and put his hands inside her shirt. "The eroticism is very subtle here."

No matter what roles they played, at the end of the night they merged in the bed. They even began to look alike.

"If I were a boy I'd be you," Alicia said.

"You'd be wilder."

She cut her hair and wore his shirts. The shirts smelled musky, like sweat and like sandalwood soap, like him or like them, she wasn't sure. Sometimes she put eyeliner on him and he looked prettier than she did. Men in the Castro stared. Leather-chapped chaps and pale, pierced boys with blue hair.

Then Alicia gained a few pounds from all the Sunday croissants that left buttery stains on the napkins, the Kahlua-and-milks, and from the birth control pills she had started to take. She dug her nails into the unfamiliar flesh—the breasts, the hips. It was like they belonged to another girl. Peter stayed so thin.

Once, near the end of the semester, she broke an empty gin bottle—threw it to the floor and felt it shatter as if it were a part of her, as if the bones in her wrist were glass splintering. Peter held her, hunching his shoulders to shield her, and she choked on her tears, squeezing her belly, disgusted by the extra pounds that had lumped themselves there.

Alicia and Peter moved in together a few weeks after that. It was June. They shared the tiny glass cube at the end of the house, filling it with things they had collected—old Velvet Underground, Chopin, Hendrix, X, and T. Rex on vinyl, books of Frank O'Hara, John Donne and Emily Dickinson, posters of Klimt and Picasso's Blue Period, a wine bottle filled with dried flowers, a plastic dove from the bins of a five-and-dime store.

Alicia went off the pill and started to lose weight.

While Peter was at work, she lay in the garden sun, letting the warmth burn into her. She waited for Peter to come home; there was no one else she thought of spending time with. On weekends they took drives to the country, jogged in the hills, went to museums, read poetry in cafe's, took photographs of each other. There was a slowness about them. They didn't stay up late anymore, sawdust whispers over wine, beat-love-poetry all night.

By the end of the summer something was changing. Peter seemed preoccupied, distant, staring into his coffee or his book. After they made love, they slept apart. The single bed seemed too small for the first time. Alicia would turn away and fill her lungs with air. Peter ground his teeth in his sleep.

When they went out, Alicia noticed all the women, wishing she were tall like that, blond like that. Her eyes darted from the women to Peter.

She was not getting her period, so she went to the doctor for a pregnancy test.

"You're not pregnant," the doctor said. "Have you been eating?"

She told Peter that night, "I think I'm really sick."

He didn't say anything, just looked at her with glazed eyes. She wanted him to say, "Oh baby, it'll be okay. We'll take care of it." It was what her father would have said. She wanted him to take her out to dinner and order brown rice and vegetables and white wine.

That night they lay in the darkness and she shivered; her stomach growled.

"Peter," she whispered.

He sighed. "What's wrong?"

"I can't sleep. I feel weak."

"You should eat something, then," he said.

He turned his back to her. Alicia curled up, her head under the covers, wondering what it was she wanted from him.

She heard the grind of molars next to her in the bed.

Now, Alicia heard Peter hesitating outside of their door before he came in. He put on the light. It burned her eyes like a chemical. The rain had darkened his hair, pressed it against his skull, and his eyelashes were starred with wet. He held roses in his nervous hands.

Alicia hated the roses. She hated the pink wet roses he was holding. The flowers reminded her of the morning she woke up to a quilt covered with flowers he had stolen from the neighborhood. The way they had made love, crushing petals until the whole room smelled of pollen and sex. They reminded her of his wounded-looking mouth as he read his poems.

Peter handed her the roses and took off his jacket. The water had gone through to his shirt so that it stuck to his thin shoulders and chest. He was the same white as his shirt.

"Thank you for the flowers, Peter," Alicia said in the voice she knew he hated. She sounded perfectly controlled. She put the roses down beside her, trying to keep in mind exactly what she was going to tell him.

"I have to talk to you," she said.

Peter sat on the narrow bed with her. She could smell the rain that had soaked into him and she could see how blue his eyes were. She tried not to think of how she kissed those eyes, how the eyelids trembled when he came.

"I'm going home. I dropped out of school today. My mom and dad are coming to get me tomorrow. I'm sorry I didn't tell you first but I realized that I've got to get out of here. I need to be with my dad now."

She had not told the psychiatrist about Peter. She had not told the psychiatrist about her father. He had been diagnosed with cancer just before she went away to school. They had treated him, and now there was more. But he was going to come get her, anyway. He was going to get in the car with her mother, even though it hurt him to sit for too long, and drive up and bring her home. On the phone last night he had waited until she stopped crying and said, "There's only one condition. We're going to stop for Foster's Freeze ice cream on the way. And you know I hate eating dessert alone."

The night she first made love with Peter she had started crying while he was still inside her. She had wanted to ask him if he could feel the crying in himself, then.

"My dad has cancer," she had said.

And he had just held her, not saying anything, until she fell asleep. A few nights later he told her that his mom had died from it, too. After going through chemo and losing her hair and a lot of weight. He couldn't remember her very well, though. He had a stepmother who had raised him like her own kid. He had shown Alicia her picture. The health shone out of her, aggressive and bright, like her bleached hair.

After that, neither of them talked about Peter's real mother or Alicia's father.

Peter just looked at Alicia now. Then he bit his lower lip and turned his head away. He made a soft, nervous sound, almost like a laugh.

"Well . . . how do you feel? You never say anything anymore."

Peter breathed hard through his nose. She saw his shoulders heave. After all this time together it was as if she could see the emotion in him—locked between his scapulae and in his sternum. He looked at her, narrowing his eyes, breathing hard.

"I love you. I just have to leave. I'm a mess. And my dad is sick." She was almost screaming. "Can't you say anything?"

"Just . . . let . . . me," Peter sounded strangled. There was a long silence of rain and breath. Alicia started to sob into her hands. He watched the sobs shaking her narrow torso. The roses were lying next to her on the bed. Some of the rainwater had soaked into the quilt.

He did not turn around but stood facing the door, his

hands forming fists, his shoulders stooped but rigid. Alicia wanted him to hold her, to take care of her, to make the pain about her dad dissolve away. She knew that this was part of what had ruined everything, but she wanted it once more, anyway. There weren't many men like her father—that kind, that strong. Maybe there weren't any. She rubbed her hands along the backs of her thighs to warm them. Then she crossed her arms on her chest and grasped her shoulders. They felt like the skulls of birds.

Finally, Peter turned. She reached up and he took her hands, warming them in his own. Then he knelt and pressed her hands under his armpits. The heat of his body made her hands ache, then tingle.

They did not make love. They had not made love for a while. They had hardly touched for a week. But that night they slept close again, Peter's hands solid heat on her abdomen.

Alicia dreamed her body was all light and shadows in yards of sheer white lace. She was standing beside Peter at the end of a corridor and he turned to her, lifting the veil that hid her face. He leaned to kiss her. She parted red lips, revealing fang-like teeth.

The next morning, Peter kissed her eyes. He took the small plastic dove off the shelf and put it into her hand. Then he left.

Alicia lay on the bed waiting for her parents to come for her.

A NOTE FROM FRANCESCA LIA BLOCK

I wrote an earlier version of "The Box" while studying creative writing and English literature at U.C. Berkeley. When David Gale asked me for a piece about being trapped, I immediately thought of the story and the feelings I had experienced at that time in my life.

I am the author of nine books including the five award-winning Weetzie Bat books, *The Hanged Man,* and *Girl Goddess #9—Short Stories.* Currently I am working on a new title for Joanna Cotler at Harper Collins.

My work has opened up all kinds of unexpected doors. It has introduced me to inspiring people and taken me to places I might never have otherwise seen. For example, I recently interviewed Tori Amos at her recording studio in England for *SPIN* magazine. My writing has also brought with it the surprising honor of being named one of *BUZZ* magazine's "100 Coolest People in L.A." for 1996. I feel very grateful to be able to share my stories and connect to others in this way.

At times in my life I have felt trapped; writing stories like "The Box" helps release me from emotional confinement. I hope that my readers will find some sense of freedom as well.

. . . *many had tried to break the ice, or break the Princess within. Some had wanted her restoration; others, her destruction. They'd brought artillery barrages, air assaults, every manner of bomb or wrecker to the grove, only to leave behind craters, burns, and waste—and a Princess untouched, forever in her ice.*

"*That's* some *ice,*" said Pugnacious.

Grinder nodded.

"*She's really alive in there?*"

THE WOEFUL PRINCESS

BY DAVID SKINNER

There are places sideways of the Earth, and to one of these places Pugnacious Footefake went.

He did not go willfully. He went accidentally. Regarding his sudden trip to there, he had only one initial thought, one he cast for himself as a rule: Never—but never—when you are walking to work and carrying your lunch in a sack—*never* blink, sneeze, and belch all at once; otherwise you will end up sideways of the Earth.

Whether his blink-sneeze-belch was indeed *the* cause of his sudden trip, Pugnacious didn't know. It seemed as reasonable a cause as any.

Pugnacious knew he was not in his town of Flattened Hills anymore because there were no streets, no curbs, no sidewalks, no cars, no shops, no signs, nor any traffic lights. No pedestrians, either. There was snow, however, crusted by ice, more furiously white than the sun above. And black etching trees in the distance. And a rude amount of cold.

At first, Pugnacious was merely annoyed, since clearly

he'd be late for work. (He had planned to open his shoe store at nine o'clock today.) Then he noticed he had no boots. Had no gloves. Had no hat. Had no coat. Had no warmth.

"Oww," he said. "I'm freezing."

Speaking was a bad idea. The air ferried ice to his lungs. He felt his nose hairs becoming stone, his cheeks becoming glass.

The snow was up to his knees.

Move, he thought.

No—Blink.

Sneeze.

Belch.

Blink. Sneeze. Belch.

Pray.

Blinksneezebelch.

Can't!

No good.

Move.

Walk.

Toward the trees. Why not?

Walking was barely that. More like churning the snow with his legs. Churning and churning and tumbling forward and slapping on the ice. Cracks in the ice webbed out from his fall. Angrily he wanted to hurl his lunch, just because; but he kept his only food, stuffing it, in its sack, into his shirt. He thought of fires, gigantic fires, uncontrolled conflagrations devouring those distant trees and encircling him with heat, and he felt ashamed. Pugnacious, you see, was not only owner of a shoe store—he was chief of the volunteer fire department; and it's simply shameful when a fire chief longs for fires. . . .

Presently his throat was barren. He was thirsty, on top of everything else. He considered the can of pop in his sack, but his hands were already too frozen to hold it, let alone open it. So he scooped up some snow, a mound into the stiff cup of his hands, and let it take some more of his warmth—so that it would melt a little; and then he ate it. He didn't know if that was a good idea. It seemed just the sort of commonsense thing that experts always warned against. Or was he thinking of something else, like drinking seawater when you are in a lifeboat, lost?

In any event, as Pugnacious let the snow wet his throat, the Princess spoke sadly to him.

You're cold.

Or rather, there was a tingling in Pugnacious that said a million things to him, to his fingernails and earlobes, to his kneecaps and shoulders; but right then the clearest of the million was that sympathetic remark made to his heart.

You're cold.

And within Pugnacious the remark was not just a pair of words. He no longer pictured his shoe store, closed for good, with a pathetic sign on its door: CLOSED FOR GOOD—PROPRIETOR FROZE TO DEATH. In fact he saw himself surrounded by people wildly desiring his shoes and also promising, in the most heartening spirit of fire safety, never to overburden their electric outlets. The remark, so sympathetic, had make his hope far less barren.

And so Pugnacious was feeling almost chipper when, a few minutes after his drinking of the Princess, he died.

Not Heaven.

Only the familiar snow. Yet against this rage of white was something unfamiliar—a smoldering of black: a punk in leather. The punk was prodding Pugnacious with a rifle. Pugnacious was on his back.

So Pugnacious hadn't died. That was irksome. If you felt that you had died, then by all that was just, you should be dead. You should not still be alive.

"Who are you?"

"Grinder," answered the punk. He spoke through the scarf that was wrapped around his lower face. "Stand up already."

Pugnacious tried. At least he got vertical; but he was still knee-deep in the snow.

"How could you end up like that, anyhow?"

In reply, Pugnacious only glowered at the punk.

"Don't you have snowshoes?"

Pugnacious thought, *Wingtips, loafers, high-tops, sandals* . . . No, he did not have snowshoes. Not in his store and not, right then, on his feet.

"He doesn't have snowshoes," muttered the punk in disbelief as he clamped a hand on Pugnacious's elbow and lifted him up onto the ice.

Once he was on the ice, Pugnacious yanked his elbow away.

Grinder was alone, like Pugnacious, but much more suitably dressed. He was an outlaw of sorts—a solemn and restless kid, that is, who had a gun. Grinder indeed had a gun, a military rifle, slick and unfriendly. And with his gun and with his attitude, Grinder loitered outside the laws.

Not that there were so many laws or that Grinder had ever broken any of them. But he did disdain the laws a whole lot and point his gun at things.

Today, Grinder actually let off a round. He shot the sun as he snarled, so that Pugnacious was intimidated. The wounding of the sun, and the sight of Grinder's teeth, did not have no effect. But more than anything else Pugnacious was still just cold and had no time for being intimidated. He asked for water. He asked for a coat, or better, a blanket. He asked to be taken far from the snow, to wherever it was dry.

"No such place," said Grinder.

Pugnacious repeated his requests.

Somewhat grudgingly, Grinder took his extra clothing from his pack. Pugnacious dressed himself as well as he could: He was still generally numb, and Grinder's clothes weren't quite big enough for him; but he managed. Grinder gave him a scarf and a blanket. Pugnacious wrapped his face in the scarf and himself in the blanket. From Grinder's canteen, Pugnacious took a drink. Then he wearily sat down, even though Grinder advised him not to.

Grinder looked at Pugnacious. He suddenly realized how out of place Pugnacious was. Pugnacious was not only underdressed; he seemed at odds with the field that held him. Grinder looked back along Pugnacious's tortured, churned-up path, right back to the horizon, and saw, to his astonishment, that the path *began* in the snow . . .

Grinder wasn't the mystical sort, despite what had happened to the Princess. But it was clear that Pugnacious had descended from the sky. Either that, or he had ascended from within the Earth. Or else he had been standing in the field before the snows had come and had only now, a hundred years later, decided it was too cold to stay any longer.

Likelihood, in any event, seemed to have passed Pugnacious by, and this set Grinder to thinking. Unlikely events meant a coming apart of accepted things. Change was possible.

In the blanket Pugnacious dozed. Using the blanket as a sledge, Grinder dragged Pugnacious across the icy field. He took him through shallower snow, toward the grove of the Princess.

Pugnacious resented being dragged. Soon after he awoke he got himself out of the blanket sledge and, despite his weakness, walked the rest of the way. His feet didn't sink as much as before, since the snow wasn't as deep, but he had to resist a powerful wish to fall down. He shivered a lot. He complained about his shivering. Grinder told him to be quiet.

They reached the grove. Hidden at its edge was a large bundle. "My tent and equipment," said Grinder. "I take it down whenever I leave for a while. We'll put it up later, if we have to."

"Why not put it up now?"

"Other things to do."

"Like what?"

Grinder merely gestured into the grove.

Pugnacious looked around. At first he did not suppose there was anything special about the grove. But then he began to wonder.

Throughout the grove were stumps and blasted trees and scattered hunks of metal. Pugnacious made out the shapes of springs, gears, rods, and other mechanical debris, all dusted white with snow. It seemed that there had been explosions and fires, some recently, some long ago, all of them focused on a lonely and peculiar mass of ice.

Pugnacious asked, "What exactly happened here?"

After a moment Grinder replied, "So you don't know."

"No."

"Hm."

"Well?"

"Oh. A bunch of little battles."

"There were *battles* here?"

"Sometimes. Mostly just attacks."

"Attacks on what?"

"That ice over there."

"That lump of ice?"

"Yeah."

"Why would anyone attack a lump of ice?"

"The Princess is in there."

"What Princess?"

"*The* Princess. She's in there."

Pugnacious squinted. "I don't see anyone."

"The ice is thick."

"But someone's in there."

"Yeah. The Princess."

Pugnacious frowned. "So she's dead."

"No."

"Asleep."

"No."

"Awfully cold."

Grinder glared at Pugnacious. "Don't make jokes."

"I wasn't making a joke. It looks cold in there."

Grinder paused. "It is."

"So she's alive?"

"Yeah."

"How could she possibly be alive?"

"Who knows. But she is."

"Oh. Well, why is she in the ice?"

Grinder didn't say.

"Don't you know?"

He wouldn't say.

Pugnacious huffed. "Fine. *Be* that way. *Don't* tell me."

Grinder just stared at him.

"Okay, okay. So people have attacked the ice. Do they want the Princess out of there?"

"Yeah, some people do."

"Hurrah! You answered my question. Thank you *so* much."

Grinder gave him a vile look.

Pugnacious sighed. "Why is this Princess so important?"

Grinder didn't answer right away. Pugnacious thought that Grinder was getting tight-lipped again. He was about to snap at him when Grinder drew a breath and, answering Pugnacious, explained the importance of the Princess.

The world's government, said Grinder, had been healthy enough, a hundred years before; and the Princess, in the normal course of things, was to become Ruler of All. But then a terrible winter struck the world. The Princess was encased in a seemingly invincible ice. These were acts of some Dark Malevolence, or so some people cried; in any event, with the Princess all but gone and the world tipping into hysteria, the government just couldn't hold. It burst. The royal family, their daughter in ice, never ended their grief, and merely sat by as their power was seized by the ever underhanded Ministry of State. This Bureaucrats' Coup insulted the highborn elite, who chose to rebel; but the Rebellion of the Aristocrats achieved little more than the execution of a million Ministers and clerks, and ever since then the government had been a shambles. Despots, democrats, royal pretenders—all came; and all went.

No one who sought control could claim any sort of *right* to control, and so their regimes would fail. Perhaps things might have been otherwise had the Princess simply died. Yet she hadn't died. Though frozen, she lived, and everyone knew this. And most agreed that the chaos and the winter would never end until either the Princess was restored to her rightful throne—or she was finally destroyed.

Therefore many had tried to break the ice, or break the Princess within. Some had wanted her restoration; others, her destruction. They'd brought artillery barrages, air assaults, every manner of bomb or wrecker to the grove, only to leave behind craters, burns, and waste—and a Princess untouched, forever in her ice.

"That's *some* ice," said Pugnacious.

Grinder nodded.

"She's really alive in there?"

"Yes."

"How do you know she's alive?"

"They've detected a heartbeat, brain waves, the usual. Besides, she's talked to a few people. Sort of."

"Talked to people? How can she *talk* to people?"

Grinder shrugged. "Different ways. Through the wind, through the trees, through the snow. She's kind of seeped into the countryside."

Through the snow?

Pugnacious whispered, "I've heard her."

"What? You have?"

"Yeah. I drank some snow."

"And then you heard her."

"Yes."

Grinder was surprised. So Pugnacious had heard the Princess—yet *another* unlikelihood. It really was time for things to come apart. Grinder just knew it.

"I've heard her, too," said Grinder. "Few people have." He tightened the clothing around himself. "Come on. Let's free her."

Pugnacious blinked. "Free her? How?"

Grinder shrugged. "You tell me."

Everyone knew the grove's location. But for several years there had been no political firestorms—the tourists and the pilgrims seldom came—the grove was generally undisturbed. The silence and twilight had settled comfortably there.

A few months after running away from home, Grinder had come to the grove. Out of curiosity. Out of boredom with the road. He had been to the grove during a vacation with his family, ages before. He'd also been to the Canyon and to the Falls.

In the grove he shot the ice twenty times, just to see how invincible it really was. It didn't even chip. The bullets ricocheted.

Then he stared out at the field. He decided that after all his traveling and gunplay, he needed a drink. His canteens, however, were empty; he'd forgotten to refill them, having left the last town in something of a hurry. And so, just as Pugnacious would, Grinder melted some snow and drank it. . . .

He and the Princess did not really converse as the weeks went by. They could say a few things to each other, but never *with* each other. Their daydreams mingled, they listened, they saw. But they couldn't quite converse.

Inevitably Grinder wondered how the Princess could be freed. He sensed that she knew a way, or suspected a way, but wasn't going to tell him, or couldn't tell him. It seemed to be up to Grinder to free her—yet he didn't have a single untried idea.

He stayed, at least, and this pleased them both. Once in a while he had to leave to get supplies, but he always returned. And he never left until he had to. Sometimes he was down to nothing but water.

The water, of course, never ran out. All of his water came from the snow.

* * *

"The thing is," said Grinder, "that for a hundred years, men better equipped than you or I have tried to melt that ice."

In fact, everything short of nuclear weapons had been used. Nuclear strikes *had* been ordered, but coups and revolutions had always prevented the orders from being carried out. And in any event there was a popular disinclination to nuke the Princess, whatever the benefit might be.

"But I know," Grinder went on, "that tonight the ice will be melted. The Princess will be freed."

"And then she'll rule the world."

Grinder winced. "No, not that. Who cares who rules? She doesn't want to rule anything."

"Then why free her?"

"That should be obvious."

"Maybe. Why is she in there?"

Grinder hesitated.

"Can't you tell me?"

"Well . . ."

"Look, I asked you this before. *Why the ice?* Where did it come from? If we free her, does that, like, pull out some support or something? Will the world blow up? I don't want to blow up. A fiery apocalypse does *not* attract me. I don't like fires. I mean, I *really* don't. A lot."

"None of that will happen."

"How do you know?"

"Because I know why she's in there."

"Why?"

"Because."

"Yes?"

Grinder paced. "She's only told *me*."

"Only you?"

"Yeah. Although she didn't really *tell* me. It's hard to explain how I know. It was just there for me to see. But *only* me. If you know what I mean."

"So it's a secret."

"Sort of."

"Tell me."

Grinder stopped pacing and sighed.

He told Pugnacious that the Princess had never wanted to be Queen of the World. When her parents retired and she alone had to take their place, she refused. She was not a happy Princess and the prospect of ruling dismayed her. No one would credit her fears, however. Everyone told her she was just being childish. *Accept it,* they said, for she would be Queen and that was that.

She was ignored. So she left the palace and came to the grove, where there was no one to ignore her. Her spirit was lifeless—*arctic,* you might even say. In her unhappiness she wished that just once, everybody—the entire world!— could feel as barren as she did then. Then she began crying, and cried a great deal, and her tears turned to ice as the world, fulfilling her wish, fell into an arctic mood.

"So this is all *her* fault? The cold and the snow?"

"Don't blame her like that. She didn't *expect* her wish to come true. It just did. Wishes sometimes do. Sometimes in a *very* big way."

"And her tears? The ice is her *tears?*"

Grinder nodded.

Pugnacious scratched his head. After a moment he cried out, with some exasperation, "Well, what else do you do with tears, but wipe them away?" He stomped up to the Princess, took off his glove, and drew his hand across the surface of the ice. The tears wet his palm. And as a warming wind arose and the ice became transparent, he was able at last to see the face of the woeful Princess.

She was smiling. Gratefully.

Afterward, there was summer.

The people had of course recognized the Princess, since her photo was in every textbook and weekly in every tabloid; and they'd not doubted her identity because, as all could see, the winter was gone and the grove was empty. Everyone gladly gave the Princess authority over them all.

This time she did not refuse the throne. She became Queen without argument, for she had heard of the past century's chaos and wished at all costs to prevent its return. She accepted her role despite all its difficulties.

Her only friends at first were Grinder and Pugnacious. She wanted nothing to do with her family's descendants, who were strangers after all. What's more, while she had been frozen she had spoken to only a few people, and all of them had passed away—except, of course, for Grinder and Pugnacious, who were, therefore, her only friends.

She and Grinder even sort of fell in love, as you might have expected. Their courtship was peculiar. It didn't work out, and not merely because he was sixteen and she was almost a hundred years older. She hadn't in fact aged, but the world around her had; and that was Grinder's world. She was a Queen, he was a punk. After about a year they took leave of each other.

During that time and for decades beyond, Pugnacious lived in the palace as a cherished guest. Right up to the end the Queen had never, in her mind, properly repaid Pugnacious for freeing her. She offered him everything, most of which he didn't really want. There was one thing she had wanted to give him all along but she withheld it, because it somehow seemed too simple—and she knew, besides, that Pugnacious, being Pugnacious, might have been embarrassed.

But one day, after they had grown old together and become so used to each other's ways, the Queen finally gave him the gift she had withheld. Her decision, and her act, had been made not a moment too soon, for the next day Pugnacious was gone.

You see, as he shambled along the street, returning from the market with some bread (he refused to eat any food bought for him by royal servants), Pugnacious blinked, sneezed, and belched, all at once. He went sideways again, to a place twice sideways of the Earth—you could say, above the Earth; but as he went he recalled the kiss the Queen had given him the day before, on his palm that had wiped away her tears.

And her kiss kept him warm.

A NOTE FROM DAVID SKINNER

I was born in 1963; I remember watching live TV coverage of the first steps on the moon, and I was very glad when disco died (although it came back, zombielike, as "dance music"). I became a writer because writing was the one art form that required no training or expensive tools.

Pugnacious Footefake was born in 1982 and was the only survivor of a novel that crashed. Since then he has surfaced in several of my stories—some for kids, some not. I am grateful that Pugnacious, although he is annoyed by magical situations, nonetheless saved the Woeful Princess; and I am grateful that the Woeful Princess was so kind to Pugnacious, since I know he could use such kindness.

The wind whistled past the doorway, every once in a while punching through, peppering his face with sand and ash and cinders. Hector barricaded his face from the wind with his backpack.

He lay for what seemed like hours, hoping the raging fire wouldn't notice him if he were quiet enough. At times he seemed to doze off, only to be wakened by questions. Would he ever leave this room? Would his parents ever get over their grief if he died?

FOUNTAIN OF YOUTH

BY MARC TALBERT

When Jonathan stepped to the side of the trail, fumbling with the front of his jeans, Hector gave him a little privacy, turning toward what should have been a creek on the other side of the trail. Even though it hadn't rained for months, he and Jonathan hadn't expected the canyon to be so dry. The stream was nothing more than a few pools, easily mistaken for the shadows of boulders and rocks littering the streambed. There was more running water splattering behind Hector than in the entire canyon.

When the splattering stopped, Hector turned to see Jonathan zipping up and grinned. "That you, or the Fountain of Youth?"

"Both," said Jonathan. "Now that I got rid of my youth, I wanna talk like a man, walk like a man . . . you know." He looked at his watch. "Take a break? Can't be more than a couple hours to the visitors center, even if we crawl around those ruins—what d'you call 'em? Ceremonial Cave?—you know, the ones we missed on the way up."

Hector nodded. He walked to nearby log and dropped

bottom, leaning forward so he didn't tip backward onto the pack that hung like a dead thing from his back. It was half as full as when they'd started three days ago, but felt twice as heavy.

The log shuddered as Jonathan sat. "Be glad to get back?"

Hector nodded. "It's been fun, though."

"Yeah." Jonathan paused. "Hey, thanks for not freaking out, man . . . last night."

"That's okay. What're friends for?"

"You're a real pal, ya know?"

Hector nodded and let his eyes drift up the wall of the canyon, looming nearly a thousand feet. Looking at the sky teetering on the cliff's edge made him as dizzy as he'd felt when Jonathan told him that his girlfriend, Julie, was pregnant and wanted to keep the baby. "I shoulda known!" Jonathan had growled. "Trapped! Next thing you know, She'll be wanting to get married and I'll have to find a job, settle down. How'm I gonna finish school, man . . . or get my GED? I'll be changing diapers and wiping up baby puke and . . ."

As he'd talked, Jonathan had thrown log after log on the fire, which seemed to fuel both his anger and the flames. "Which time was it, anyway . . . when I became a father?"

Hector couldn't help himself—picturing Jonathan and Julie in shadows that make it difficult to know which arm or leg belonged to whom. He'd stared at the fire, hoping the flames would make these pictures shrink, retreat, just as they kept wild animals at bay.

Hector looked down from the cliff to Jonathan. "The weather's been great," he said, reaching under his pack to scratch, wanting to change the subject.

"Yeah," said Jonathan. "No rain. No mosquitoes."

Hector nodded and looked up the canyon. "Might not last, though." He pointed.

Jonathan turned to look at the top of a cloud showing above the trees. "We'd better scram," he said. "If it's raining hard up there, could be a flash flood comin' down this canyon."

Hector nodded. He'd heard stories of water crashing through canyons like this one, snapping trees, herding boulders. As he got to his feet he thought he heard a rumbling from up the canyon. Thunder? Boulders bouncing off canyon walls?

Jonathan rushed down the trail, taking steps so big, they looked as if they hurt. As Hector struggled to keep up, more rumbling came from the head of the canyon, louder now.

"Jeeze," Jonathan grunted. "Must be movin' *fast!*"

Hector looked over his shoulder. The cloud loomed closer, boiling upward. As he watched, a plume shot up, off to the side, looking like flood waters hitting a canyon wall, spouting.

"Wow!" It just slipped out, loud enough so Jonathan

stopped to see what was going on. He looked over Hector's head and his face froze. "My God!" he said. "Look at that sucker!" He looked at Hector with frightened eyes. "We gotta *move!*"

They bolted down the trail. The rumbling became steady. The air seemed to twitch before it became a steady breeze, hitting them in the face instead of coming from the approaching storm. Even stranger, it wasn't the moist breeze of a storm, smelling of rain. It was dry, warm one moment and cool the next.

Although it was morning, dusk seemed to be falling. Hector tried moving his feet fast enough to keep up with the pounding of his heart. He stared at the trail, trying to make out rocks and roots that were becoming difficult to see, swatting at debris the wind tossed in his face.

"What the hell . . ." Jonathan stopped and pointed to the trail.

Hector saw what looked like a gray moth. As he looked, the breeze picked it up and sent it tumbling clumsily, moth-like, toward Hector. Hector reached out to catch it, and it crumbled in his hand.

"Ash!" Jonathan said, staring at the smudge in Hector's palm.

Hector looked at the sky. Bits of ash fluttered down. The sky sat askew, like a tarnished lid over the canyon, and the cloud seemed like steam, forcing itself under the lid, lifting.

Jonathan gasped and Hector dropped his gaze. As if from nowhere, a deer rushed toward them from up the canyon, tail up, eyes crazy with fear. It passed so closely, Hector felt its breath on the back of his arm. Another followed. And another.

What looked like a cigarette butt fell, glowing, onto the path.

Jonathan nudged it with the toe of his shoe. "Cinder! Must be a forest fire!" He shouted. "Think we're near Ceremonial Cave?"

Hector shrugged. "If we are, it's gotta be over there." He pointed across the streambed, down the canyon. Jonathan nodded, and both boys cut across the streambed, dodging around river rocks.

The juniper and piñon hid the base of the canyon wall. Scrambling up a shoulder of scree, an elk spooked them as it bolted toward the streambed. For the first time, Hector smelled smoke. Was the fire catching up to them? Where was the cave? He struggled to look down the blank canyon wall, at the same time trying to keep from stumbling over loose rock.

Up ahead, Hector saw what looked like the limbless skeletons of several toppled ponderosas, leaning against the canyon wall. As they approached he saw they were a series of lashed-beam ladders. Ceremonial Cave? A porcupine waddled from the brush. It didn't flinch or pause as Jonathan leaped over it.

"Look!" Hector shouted over the fire's roar.

Jonathan's legs churned faster, sending scree tumbling. The ladder shuddered as he leaped onto it.

Hector scrambled after Jonathan. Both the smell of smoke and the sound of fire grew stronger as they climbed the second ladder. Hector glanced up the canyon, over the trees. The cloud glowed, as if the sun had spun out of control, careening north instead of west, crashing into the earth. Flames seemed to march toward him, like torches carried by a formation of soldiers.

Hector threw himself over the top of the last ladder, landing next to Jonathan on the cave's lip. From the cave's mouth came the musty smell of dried bat guano and mouse turds.

Toward the cave's throat were square piles of rock. Behind this rubble were square doorways leading to storerooms that the ancient Anasazi had carved into the soft, pumicelike stone of the back wall. It was toward one of these doorways the boys scrambled.

The room felt small, but Hector didn't know if it was darkness or rock that pressed in on him. He sat for a moment, catching his breath. The room's air was still, and his unwashed body felt like a hot light bulb giving off stink instead of light.

"Should be safe in here." Hector nodded in the direction of Jonathan's voice. He shrugged off his backpack and leaned it against the wall.

It was then Hector felt the presence of something else in the room. He looked around, trying to stare through darkness. As his eyes became more used to the dark, he saw several lumps that could have been rocks piled in the room's back corner. Slowly, these rocks took on the remarkable likeness of a cougar. And then, as if in a dream, the likeness lifted its head and stared back at him.

Hector was unable to look away. "Jonathan!" His whisper was urgent.

"What!"

"Look. Back there." He pointed, turning Jonathan to face the right direction.

When Jonathan saw, he grunted, as if someone had punched him in the gut. The cougar stared with glazed eyes, as if he, too, might be dreaming. "Let's get outta here!" Jonathan's voice trembled.

Trying not to make sudden moves, they backed out the doorway, dragging their backpacks in front of them. Just before Hector lost sight of the cougar, it lowered its head. He backed from the opening, almost stepping on a pack rat scampering into the room they'd just escaped.

As Jonathan peered into the next doorway, he tossed rocks inside. "This one's empty," he shouted, crawling.

Before joining his friend, Hector looked up the canyon. The fire shone through billows of smoke, leaping from treetop to treetop. Pockets of the air itself seemed to be burning. The fire's roar vibrated through his body, and his ears rattled with the sound. Several at a time, tree crowns burst into flames, quick as struck matches. It was at once the most terrifying and beautiful thing Hector had ever seen. As branches fell, the tallest trees became flagpoles, the wind whipping and shredding the unfurled ribbons of flame.

Across the canyon, he saw a darker shape swirling in and out of smoke. With swimming movements, it was climbing a giant ponderosa. A bear. As Hector watched, fire leapt onto a nearby tree and from there to the bear's tree. Within seconds, the bear was aflame, seeming to swell with fire, clinging to the trunk, its mouth scissoring open and closed toward the sky, its cries of pain loud enough to be heard over the fire's roar and the huge pops of trees exploding and branches dropping like bombs. Hector cried out. Shutting his eyes, he dove into the opening through which Jonathan had disappeared. Smoke was almost as thick inside the room as out. And the air was growing hot enough to make breathing uncomfortable.

He stumbled into Jonathan before he saw him. Spooked, Jonathan raised his arms protectively, as if Hector were the cougar. "I don't wanna *die!*" he moaned. "I don't wanna *die!*"

"Me neither," Hector said, growing faint. He wanted more air, but the air was too smoky and hot to breathe deeply. His fingers were tingling now, and his throat felt stretched tight, as if his head were floating, straining against its tether of neck.

"I *can't* die. I'm gonna be a *father!*" Jonathan moaned.

Hector slumped onto the cave's floor. Jonathan's sobs were soon overwhelmed by the fire's roar. The constant popping outside sounded like guns on a TV. Hector's lungs ached from smoke, but he forced himself to breathe slowly and evenly.

The wind whistled past the doorway, every once in a while punching through, peppering his face with sand and ash and cinders. Hector barricaded his face from the wind with his backpack.

He lay for what seemed like hours, hoping the raging fire wouldn't notice him if he were quiet enough. At times he seemed to doze off, only to be wakened by questions. Would he ever leave this room? Would his parents ever get over their grief if he died?

At times, he felt that he was hallucinating. Was he being cooked in an oven or microwave? Would the cougar like him rare or well done? It felt at times as if the wind outside was tamping the smoke inside, packing it solid, mummifying him for future archaeologists to puzzle over, dissect, carbon-date.

It was with surprise that he realized his fingers no longer tingled and that his head felt attached to his body, and was throbbing. The air, although hot, seemed cooler and less smoky.

Where was the fire's roar? Where were the sounds of trees exploding? He lifted his head and looked toward the doorway. Had night fallen? He looked at the glowing dial of his watch. It was either noon or midnight—he didn't know which.

He saw Jonathan curled up nearby. He hesitated to touch him, fearing his friend was dead. Gently, his hand trembling, he nudged Jonathan's shoulder. To Hector's relief, Jonathan groaned, stirring.

"I think it went past us," Hector croaked.

Jonathan pulled himself up, sitting, and shook his head. "Jeeze! Feels like a hangover!"

"Let's get outta here."

Jonathan groaned as he crawled toward the doorway, dragging his backpack with one hand.

When he stepped outside, Hector tried not to look at the tree with the bear. He couldn't help himself. If he hadn't known it was a bear, he wouldn't have been able to tell. It still clung to the tree, charred and black, welded to wood, charred and black. His eyes strained to cry but were too dry for tears. He forced himself to look over the lip of the cave.

The first two ladders had been burned. Only the top one was still standing, although one side of it looked scorched. "I don't trust the way this ladder looks," Hector said.

Jonathan nodded. "Let's throw our packs down . . . try climbing." The smoke eddying below make the packs look as if they were sinking in water.

For a few minutes, they studied the canyon wall at their feet. It was like trying to figure out a maze, following a possible path with their eyes only to bump into a dead end.

"Over there." Jonathan pointed. "Toe- and hand-holds."

Sure enough, Hector saw a series of evenly spaced dents in the rock, right-left-right-left, slanting down from near the top of the ladder. Hector went first, hugging the wall. A layer of fine ash made the rock slippery. He wished the holes were deeper and wondered several times if this was safe, if they'd eroded since the Anasazi had last used them.

After he'd guided Jonathan down, they collapsed.

"Man!" Jonathan said. "We were lucky to be close to that cave . . . those ruins."

Hector nodded. "We'd better get going."

They found their backpacks and checked for fire before putting them on. The smoldering ground was hot enough to feel through the soles of their shoes.

As they walked toward the stream, what looked like a wild turkey came hopping out of a tangle of charred underbrush. It was hopping, but had no feet. It was opening its mouth to cry, but no sound came out. It flapped its wings, almost bare except for a few scorched feathers. All over its pimply flesh were oozing burns. It bumped into a stump and continued its blind dance in the other direction.

Hector doubled over as his stomach tried turning

inside out. He was surprised by how much food it had been holding.

The wild turkey was the worst. But as they struggled over and under toppled, blackened trees, they saw the bodies of many animals. Some, especially birds, were unburned, as if they'd been overcome by smoke and fallen from the sky after the fire had done its worst. Some were blackened shapes, blistered shadows of whatever they had been. Hector stepped over what he thought was a small tree branch, only to see a snake's head attached to one end. The smell of scorched flesh told them they were near an animal even when they couldn't see it.

Dry as the riverbed had been before, it was steaming now. All the puddles had boiled dry, a few of them leaving behind trout and salamander, the flesh partly cooked off their bodies.

Dazed and silent, they found the trail and turned left, walking toward the visitors center. The scorched body of a horny toad, shaped like a serrated arrowhead, pointed the way, its legs burned off.

They may have gone one mile or two. Either way it felt like ten.

Hector heard the voices first, coming from down the trail.

"Hey!" he shouted, his voice cracking.

The voices stopped. And then came a call. "Hello! Anybody there?"

"Here!" Hector and Jonathan shouted at the same time. They began stumbling down the trail, lurching, dazed as the deer they'd seen earlier.

"Whoa!" said a man, catching Hector in his arms.

Hector felt himself go limp.

They were farther from the visitors center than they'd both thought. They passed fire crews who were searching for embers to kill and a fire line that had been dug across the canyon, streambed and all. The fire had been diverted from the visitors center by planes dropping a slurry of fire retardants. Hector had never smelled anything quite like it before.

It seemed to take forever before Hector found himself lying on a flagstone floor as a paramedic checked him out. Jonathan was lying next to him. "That tickles!" he heard Jonathan complain.

"Must mean you're okay. Anything we can get you?"

"Water." Jonathan spoke for both of them.

A man in a ranger's uniform brought them styrofoam cups of water and a couple doughnuts each. He took a little notebook from his shirt pocket and slid a pen from its spiral binding. "We need some information from you boys so we can call your parents, tell 'em you're okay." He opened the notebook, his pen poised. "We'd let you call 'em yourselves, but things are jamming around here."

After he repeated everything they told him, he closed the notebook. "Sit tight. We need to ask you some questions . . . where you were camping, other campers you may have seen, what you saw of the fire . . . you know, that kind of thing."

They watched what was going on around them as they nibbled doughnuts and sipped water.

"It's like the emergency room at St. Vincent's . . . when I broke my arm," Hector said.

Jonathan nodded. "Looks like a car crash . . . without the cars."

There were people on radio phones, and topographical maps taped helter-skelter on walls and the windows. A woman and two men were going from one map to another, discussing the status of the fire and where the fire crews were located. When they got near, the boys scooted over, to better watch and listen.

"Hey," Jonathan whispered, nudging Hector with his elbow. "That map shows where we were camping." Hector nodded.

"We got a report from Darcey's crew," the woman said, pointing. "They came across evidence that would put the start of the fire here." She touched the map. "An untended campfire."

Hector felt Jonathan go stiff beside him.

"Damn," one of the men said. "I'd love to get my hands on the bastards who were camping there."

"We will," the woman said, her voice grim. "And when we do, they'll pay for it. One way or the other, they'll pay."

It was then that the ranger returned, carrying two Cokes. "Sorry it took so long. Your parents were mighty happy to hear you guys are okay. They'll be along soon to get you." He looked at the Cokes. "Found these. Care for some?" He held them out.

Hector was about to nod and reach when Jonathan spoke up. "Sure. But, sir, could you tell us where the men's room is?"

The ranger pointed. "Over there, second door on the right. I'll put the Cokes on this table. Don't be long. Remember, I got some questions to ask before your parents take you home."

"Stop that!" Hector hissed as Jonathan took him by the arm to hurry him along.

Once in the men's room, Jonathan turned and grabbed Hector's shoulders. "They think *our* campfire started it!" he said in a raspy whisper.

"How could it?" Hector spoke aloud, defying Jonathan to shush him. "We even pissed on it before we left."

"That's what the map lady said. Look, I don't think it did either. We buried it and pissed on it and *everything!* But it doesn't matter what *we* think. If they think we did it, there's gonna be hell to pay. And I don't want more trouble than I already got."

Hector thought of Julie. "What does *that* have to do with anything?"

"Look!" Jonathan brought his smudged face closer to

Hector's. "I'm gonna be a *father!* What kind of father lives in jail?"

"So you're gonna be a father! So? So what d'ya want me to do? Lie?"

Jonathan pulled back, closed his mouth, and nodded. "Yeah. Tell 'em we were in the next canyon over . . . Water Canyon. And that we saw a couple dudes this morning, camping near where they think the fire started."

Hector stared at Jonathan, not believing what he was hearing.

"Be a pal," Jonathan continued. "It won't do any good for them to put us in jail. What's done is done." Hector thought of the bear bursting into flames. "I just want to have a chance to . . . to do what's right for Julie and the kid." Hector thought of the wild turkey, dancing on legs with the feet burned off.

Hector felt like decking Jonathan. Instead, he turned toward the urinal and fumbled with the front of his jeans. Fountain of Youth, he thought, watching yellow beat against white.

What a creep, using a baby to bait a trap for him! It didn't seem possible that their campfire could have caused such a raging fire. But what if it had?

He zipped up and flushed, watching his youth disappear.

He turned to Jonathan, barely able to look him in the face. "Come on. Let's go talk to the ranger."

A NOTE FROM MARC TALBERT

It is unnerving to step outside one's house and see ashes falling from the sky, like incinerated pieces of cloud. It is equally unnerving to see the sun set red as blood in a sky that is so filled with smoke it looks bruised. But most unnerving is to step outside one's house after dusk, look to the west, and see patches of mountain glowing, as if the sun got stuck going down.

Forest fires are part of life around where I live. Usually they are small and controllable and not so close that they threaten the safety of my family. But several summers ago we experienced a drought so severe, I have just now grown thirsty remembering it. It was so dry that we could tell where people were hiking in the hills around our house by the clouds of powdery dust their feet kicked up. It was so dry that many of the wild bushes didn't produce leaves until August, after our first (brief) rain of the year. It was so dry that little forest fires exploded into huge fires, raging out of control, close enough so we went to bed with the smell of wood smoke in our hair and woke to the smell of wood smoke on our pillows.

The fire that inspired "Fountain Of Youth" was started by an abandoned campfire across the Río Grande Valley from my house, near Bandelier National Monument. Two young men came forward, remorsefully claiming responsibility for the campfire, wanting to do what was right by admitting their guilt. They

wanted people to know they had not set the fire inten-
tionally, that they had tried to be responsible campers,
that they had done everything most campers do to put
out campfires. Unfortunately, because of the drought,
everything they'd done wasn't enough. The buried coals
must have smoldered for several days. The wind must
have blown long and hard enough to expose them, fan-
ning them hotter even as it blew tinder onto them. The
result was a fire so hot that it burned not only tree
trunks, but the roots as well, causing firefighters to con-
tinually stumble and fall into tunnels just beneath the
surface of the charred dirt where roots had once reached
out from trees. The result was a fire so intense, it shattered rocks and boulders and turned bones to crumbs of
calcium.

Much to their surprise, the two young men were
immediately arrested.

If these young men had known they would be
arrested, would have come forward? Not being in
a position to ask them, I explored this question through
the story of Jonathan and Hector. I hope this story
describes not only the emotional, physical, and moral
traps that snared Jonathan and Hector, but sets a moral
trap for the reader as well.

What would *you* have done?
Gotcha!

. . . at first, perhaps, you will not know.
But gradually the days go by,
And hungry branches, thin and slow,
Come reaching out across the sky
And shut it from above your head.
You'll find, when you're alone at night,
You'll sense them breathing round your bed,
And through the dark without a sound
You'll feel them creeping softly round. . . .

TRAPPED

BY LOIS DUNCAN,
WRITTEN AT AGE ELEVEN

When the moonlight's shining silver
    floods the garden
You must never venture from the house
    alone
Lest the slender moonbeams bind you
    with a thread as strong as steel
And the fairy people claim you for their
    own.

They will laugh to see you struggle, they
    will frolic through your dreams,
They will find you though you spend
    your life in flight,
They will snatch you from your fireside
    and a love you'll never know,
For your heart is bound with
    moonbeams to the night.

So, on every summer's evening that the
    moon is large and full
You must close the window tight and bar
    the door.
If you huddle in an arm chair with your
    knitting or a book,
You'll be safer than you've ever been
    before.

If your eyes grow dim with star dust and
    your feet grow airy light
And your ears start ringing with a crazy
    tune,
Then you'll know you have been
    captured and your heart belongs for good
To the magic of the fairies and the moon.

TRAPPED

BY LOIS DUNCAN,
WRITTEN AT AGE THIRTEEN

There is the house where she used to live,
And there, where the rambler roses run
Up the high porch posts, is the rocking
  chair
Where she used to sit in the morning
  sun.
And there are the shades that she used to
  draw
To keep out the dark when day was
  done.
        And she was never lonely.

There is the patch of herbs she grew,
Kneeling alone in the early spring.
To break the ground still hard with cold.
And there, from the oak, hangs a broken
  swing
That was used by the children who lived
  next door
(She always said they'd break the thing).
        And she was never lonely.

There are the pictures she kept so long
Secure in a frame above her head.
And there is the clock with the cuckoo
   bird
Who mocked as the hours came and fled.
And there is the dressing gown she wore
When she stretched herself on the half
   warmed bed.
         And she was never lonely—
            She said.

TRAPPED

BY LOIS DUNCAN,
WRITTEN AT AGE SEVENTEEN

Be slow to live beside a wood
Or build your home where trees grow
  tall,
A silent, stealthy, creeping wall.
At first, perhaps, you will not know.
But gradually the days go by,
And hungry branches, thin and slow,
Come reaching out across the sky
And shut it from above your head.
You'll find, when you're alone at night,
You'll sense them breathing round your
  bed,
And through the dark without a sound
You'll feel them creeping softly round.
Sometimes by light of day you'll smile
And do some job about the place
And make yourself forget awhile,
But then a branch will brush your face,
And with a sudden gasp you'll spin
To find them slyly closing in.

Be slow to live beside a wood
Or build your home where trees grow tall,
For it can bring you nothing good—
Nothing good at all.

TRAPPED

by Lois Duncan,
written at age fourteen

We are the wise.
Do not envy us—
We who are too wise to draw near the fire
Lest we get burned;
We who are too wise to love
Lest love should vanish and we be hurt.
We are the wise.
Do not envy us our wisdom—
We who are too wise to live
Lest we should die.

TRAPPED

BY LOIS DUNCAN,
WRITTEN AT AGE SIXTEEN

Johnny will call at 8:15,
This I know for a fact.
I know exactly what Johnny will say
And just how Johnny will act.
Johnny's the sweetest guy in town,
He thinks of me night and day . . . .
(But maybe—maybe—Steve will call!
Please, dear heaven, that Steve should call!
If he happens to think of it, Steve *might* call,
    And I mustn't be away.)

Johnny will call at 8:15,
Never a moment late.
Johnny is thoughtful and fine and sweet,
Really a perfect date.
There's *always* Johnny who's awfully nice,
    (But if I sit home alone,
Maybe—maybe—Steve will call!
If there's nothing better he just might call,
And, please, dear heaven, if he *should* call
    I have to be near the phone!)

Johnny will call at 8:15,
As he always has before,
But if I leave it, the phone will ring
The moment I'm out the door.
And so, I guess, I'll stay at home
And read awhile in bed . . .
(And wait and wait for Steve to call,
And tell myself, "He still *might* call!")

Though I know damned well he'll never call
And I wish
        that
               I
                        were
                                  dead!

TRAPPED

BY LOIS DUNCAN,
WRITTEN AT AGE FORTY-TWO
FOR A SIXTEEN-YEAR-OLD DAUGHTER

There is an instant
At summer's start
When strands of springtime
Still bind the heart.
So is the moment
Each girl must know,
A time of clinging,
Then letting go.

Not quite a woman
Nor yet a child,
With plans unstable,
With dreams gone wild,
Truths grow blurry
And loved ones strange—
Oh, it is lonely
When seasons change!

A NOTE FROM LOIS DUNCAN

I started composing verse as soon as I could talk. I called those creations "porms" and would chant myself to sleep with them at night. It drove my brother, who shared the same bedroom, crazy. I can still remember the pitch of hysteria in his voice as he shouted, "Mother! Come in here and make Lois shut up!"

Later, when I learned how to read and write, I printed the "porms" in notebooks, which miraculously, I still have. All I wanted for my tenth birthday was a volume of verse by Rudyard Kipling, the master of rhyme and rhythm. I have never been particularly fond of music, which is surprising considering that both my grandmothers were concert pianists, my parents played instruments by ear, and one of my daughters sings professionally. But what the rest of my family found in melody, I found in the beat and flow of rhymed verse. That is still the case today.

It's hard to make a living writing poetry, so my career as a professional writer has centered upon other types of literature. Over three hundred of my articles and short stories have appeared in national magazines, and I am the author of over forty books, most of them young adult suspense novels. Many of those have been named American Library Association Best Books for Young Adults and Junior Library Guild Selections, and they have garnered Young Readers Awards in sixteen states and three foreign countries. My "Moment of

Glory" occurred in 1992, when I was awarded the Margaret A. Edwards Award, presented by the *School Library Journal* and the Young Adult Library Services Association to honor a living author for a distinguished body of adolescent literature.

But my heart still lurks in those "porm-filled" note-books of my youth, and when I started soliciting stories from other writers to use in this anthology, it suddenly occurred to me that a number of those poems from my early years involved one form or another of the theme "Trapped!"

So, I get to be in this book, too!

Once, he said that he knew what I was thinking, that he could tell everything I was thinking because he was my father. He only took off his belt when I had done something wrong, and to make me a better person. "You should be glad to have somebody that cares what you do!" he said. I was glad. It was like blocking off the bad parts of me, turning away the bad thoughts so that I only thought of the moment and the stinging that the belt made.

THE ESCAPE

BY WALTER DEAN MYERS

Dr. Talley was on the phone when Richie walked into his office. He looked up, smiled, and adjusted his glasses. The red tie was one Richie had seen before. There were two pictures on the back wall. The picture nearest the draped window was of a swan on a lake. The other one, the one in the center of the wall over the couch, was a gaudy arrangement of flowers. Richie stood four feet from the wall, facing away from Dr. Talley, looking at

He's on the phone again. Nobody has that many people to talk to. The same smile. He puts it on in the morning when he washes his teeth. The same stupid office, the same stupid pictures. He thinks I don't know what he's doing. I am waiting for him to get off the phone, and he is waiting for me to wait for him, thinking he will get me nervous. No, I am not nervous. I am here looking at these pictures with my back to him. I will pretend that I am interested in the swan, that the flowers turn me on as if I thought the pictures. He had seen them both a dozen times before.

"Richard, how are you today?"

Richie turned and saw Dr. Talley put the phone on the edge of the desk. He scribbled briefly in the notebook on his desk and looked up.

Richie sat where he always did, on the small couch, settling himself as Dr. Talley came around the desk to take his place on the single chair facing him. On the table between them the lamp glowed. Dr. Talley switched on the tape recorder.

"Did you catch the game yesterday?" Dr. Talley asked.

"The Yanks won," Richie said. "I didn't watch."

they were really art. That's what he wants me to do. He always wants me to do the same thing.

Richard, blow the blue away.

He smiles. What does he know? Maybe he's found something in my record. It doesn't matter. He can't see who I am, can't see beyond the skin. We are actors and this is a stage. We look at each other and pretend.

The tape recorder will know if I am lying. I know that. It will signal if I am lying. He makes sure that I see him turning it on, makes sure that if I try to get away I know I will be caught.

He slid on a patch of rain just yesterday.

His yanks on my mind don't match what I want.

He's still not sure if the yankers will ever go away. He keeps his fingers in front of his

"I'm still not sure if they're good enough to go all the way." Dr. Talley's thin hands were folded in front of his chest. "What do you think?"

Richie shrugged. He crossed his legs and quickly uncrossed them.

"At our last session you were telling me about a bluebird cup?"

"My mother used to drink out of the bluebird cups sometimes," Richie said. "When she was very tired or a little down, she would make tea and drink it out of the bluebird cups."

"What exactly is a bluebird cup?"

"It's just a regular cup but it has bluebirds on it," Richie said. "We used them on holidays, or special days like that."

chest. His nails are clean and polished and I have to look away from them. Now he folds them calmly. What do I drink?

Shrug. Water and Thorazine.

I need to be very still so he doesn't see what I am thinking, or hear my thoughts.

A sour past passion I was yelling about a two-thirds drop.

Why are we talking about the cups? He wants me to tell him that I dropped the cup. Sitting at the kitchen table all alone I thought I was so big. "You have to grow up!" My father, stinking of wine, shouted. Growing up was drinking from the good cups, but when the doorbell rang I dropped it. "What you doing?" He spit the words out at me and I looked for words to tell him, but none came. "Get in the room!"

"And you used to drink out of them, too?"

"Once."

Silence. Behind him a clock ticked on the wall. Behind Dr. Talley there was a window. Through the window, framed by the heavy curtain, was the gentle sweep of a bridge against the open sky.

"Did you want to tell me about drinking tea from a cup with a bluebird design?"

"I didn't drink tea," Richie said. "I drank milk."

"How old were you?"

"Four, maybe five."

"Did you drink tea with your . . . I'm sorry, milk, with your mother?"

"No, by myself," Richie said. "It wasn't a big deal."

"Did you do a lot of

I was already crying. In the room and taking my clothes off and I was already crying. Even before he came in with the belt. Even before the swooshing sound of the leather through the air.

The clock is staring at me. It never lasted more than three minutes. I looked at the clock; it was more than three minutes. It went on and on. I didn't want to scream. That was wrong.

Who would want to swell and steam? Me high above the sad thinking. Me flying up and up. His dark face so angry. His lips twisted and his eyes red. Drops of spit arced across the space between us as he screamed at me. "Look at me! Look at me! Why you break that cup!"

That was the worst part. The looking at him and him hating me so. He hated inside me. The belt found every part things by yourself?"

"Sometimes I would read by myself, or color. Sometimes I would just sit in my room. My mother would come in sometimes and sit with me."

"You have a sister," Dr. Talley said. "Did you share a room with her?"

"It was our room. Effie was eight. She's nineteen now and living in Seattle. I was thinking when I was eighteen I would go live with her. No, I don't think I will. I don't think I'd like Seattle."

Silence. The clock ticking away. Dr. Talley waiting for him to continue talking. Cold sweat running from his under-arms down his sides.

"Did Effie ever sit with you in your room?"

"Once in a while."

of my legs and back but only touched the outside. After-ward I trembled. I wasn't cold, but I trembled.

For the next week I sat in my room, not daring to move. Sometimes my mother came in and sat next to me.

Even if I am a mister, it didn't mean that I bared my doom to her. Or hers to me.

It was sour doom. Effie was late. She's fine/clean now, and living in Seattle.

The belt never found Effie. Sometimes he would look at her in the same awful way that he looked at me, and she would cry. But then he would come into the room at night and stand near her bed and she would pretend to be asleep. We would both pre-tend that he had not come into the room.

Dead Effie never fit with you in your gloom.

Maybe not, I don't remember."

"Richard, you seem very quiet today." Dr. Talley shifted in his seat. "Is there anything bothering you?"

"No."

"What did you think about as you sat in your room?"

"Sometimes I would think about baseball," Richie said. "I used to like the Mets and then the Yankees. I used to listen to the games after school. Effie didn't like baseball, so when she was in the room she would put music on. Always too loud. She always liked to put the radio up too loud."

Silence.

Dr. Talley's fingers drummed soundlessly on the arm of the chair.

We would sit in the dark and hope he would forget that we were there. I would think that sometimes he would remember us and think how good we were for not giving him trouble. Or sometimes I would sit in the kitchen with a glass of water before me on the table. "I am having a glass of water," I planned to say when he asked me why I was sitting and being so good, but he never asked me.

Effie would put the radio on, and I was afraid that he would think it was too loud. Mom thought it would annoy him. But he never beat Effie; he would only stand by her bed in the darkness. She would pretend to be asleep.

Dr. Talley is drumming his fingers, waiting for me to make a mistake. They have no belts here, just the demons listening to your heart beating.

Sounds from the street below drifted into the room. The honking of a horn, a whistle, a rattle. Dr. Talley leaned forward and looked directly into Richie's face, into his eyes, waiting for him to speak.

"You had some trouble in school," Dr. Talley said. "Did you think about that?"

"Sometimes."

"Tell me about the trouble."

"I was running with a compass in my hand," Richie said. "Then I fell and it went through my palm."

"And . . .?"

"And I didn't tell anybody about it because I didn't think it was a big deal," Richie said. "I thought I could put some peroxide on it, or maybe

They hear it right through your chest.

Once, he said that he knew what I was thinking, that he could tell everything I was thinking because he was my father. He could tell what Effie was thinking, too.

There was the rubble of a fool. There was a stink about it.

He only took off his belt when I had done something wrong, and to make me a better person. "You should be glad to have somebody that cares what you do!" he said.

I was glad. It was like blocking off the bad parts of me, turning away the bad thoughts so that I only thought of the moment, and the stinging that the belt made. When he had finished with me he told me to put peroxide on the place where the flesh had lifted and was sore. In the bathroom I always just cold water. I guess I should have told the nurse."

"It happened twice."

"I shouldn't have run with it."

"When kids are careless about their own safety it's often a sign that they have things on their minds," Dr. Talley said. "Did you have something on your mind at the time?"

Richie shook his head no.

"Just being in school and everything," Richie said. "No big deal."

"It became a big deal later on," Dr. Talley said. "You started staying away from school."

"Sometimes I got bored and sometimes there were other things I wanted to do." Richie sneaked a look at the clock. The door was seven to eight feet

peed first and than gently put water and peroxide on my skin without looking at myself in the mirror.

Sweet darkened lights.

The point of the compass was like a shout, like Effie turning up the radio. Once, she told me that she didn't want to hear her thoughts. I wanted to hear them, but I couldn't, and I imagined for a while that perhaps she wasn't my sister.

But then I began to realize that no matter how good I was trying to be, people were hearing the bad thoughts in my head, sometimes even before I heard them. I didn't want them listening to my thoughts, or sending notes home to him.

Sometimes I couldn't keep my mind on what was going on in school because of trying to keep out the bad thoughts.

away from the couch. The brass doorknob looked sturdy enough. Centered beneath the knob there was a round lock.

"I knew it was wrong to play hookey, but sometimes you know something and then you go on and do it, anyway," he said.

"What did your parents think when they found out?" Dr. Talley asked. "I would imagine your mother must have been concerned."

"She freaked a little. She always freaked out like that. She said I was a disgrace."

"You're smiling."

"I was just thinking about how she looked. She was fixing herself up and she smeared her lipstick all over her face. She looked funny, but I didn't tell her.

Dr. Talley was listening for the bad thoughts. There were still plenty of minutes left. If I ran for the door I could be in the hallway, unless it was locked and then he would know what I had been thinking. Maybe he would only pretend to know.

I thought of falling down on the way to school, or getting into a fight and tearing my clothes. It would have made him spitting mad.

But did your errants slink when they bound out? Fries should envision the other just have been twice burned.

She said I was a disgrace. Rue piling up into grins. Easier than her with the fear in her eyes. She holding me and rocking me so close in her arms. But she never held Effie.

"What does he do to you?" I asked Effie.

"Nothing," she would say. But there was a look on

I couldn't say anything to her because she was completely freaked."

"Then what happened?"

"Then I thought I had to get myself together. You know, get straight and stuff. You know what I thought once?"

"What?"

"That I had to get myself together," Richie said. "Then I didn't know if I had a self. That didn't make any sense, anyway."

"Did you get yourself together?"

"I'm together now," Richie said. "Right after that I got myself together. I started thinking about what I needed to do and what people wanted me to do. It was harder figuring out what everybody wanted but when I

her face that reminded me of a dog I had seen that had been hit by a car.

My mother would cry, and sometimes she would try to fix herself up, but she would always look even worse.

Then one day, I think I got shoe polish on the linoleum, I don't know, something, and he told me to go into the room. When I went in and had my pants down, I decided I wouldn't cry. He came in, his face puffed, his neck bulging, the belt wrapped around his fist.

The belt found me and I bit down and the belt whirled and slashed through the air and I could hear his curses. And it came to me then that he was the man and I was the boy and I was taking his manhood from him. Then I cried because it was what I was supposed to do. I needed to get thought about all that, it was easier to deal with stuff.

"Effie could deal with stuff. She would just smile and go on. I started dealing with stuff better, too. Only sometimes I still didn't go to school because I was thinking about the navy. I wanted to join the navy. You have to be eighteen to get into the navy, but I can wait."

"Is the navy a way of escaping?"

"No, I just wanted to travel. See different places. Maybe go to Japan, or Africa."

The green light on the tape recorder glowed faintly. Dr. Talley held his pen in the air for a long moment, then turned it gracefully between his fingers.

"You stopped going to school," Dr. Talley said.

myself together to do what people wanted me to do, to do what I was supposed to be doing. Effie could deal with stuff better than I did. She would just smile and I was fighting like I didn't know what was good for me.

I told Dr. Talley I was going to join the navy as soon as I reached eighteen.

Can real life be the same as taping?

Dr. Talley thought he could read my mind, but I looked at him and breathed out slowly so he couldn't see I was nervous. I didn't look over toward the tape machine.

A string needs to ravel, to be an indifferent race. Maybe go on a plan, or a seeker.

He said I was smart. The tests they gave me tried to find out what I was thinking. They showed me black and red figures of people being torn

"You had to know you would get into some kind of trouble. Your intelligence tests show that you're well above average and you didn't do well. What do you think about your school career and what you were doing?"

"I can make it up," Richie said. "Like you said, I can do well on tests. I can get my GED and then I'll probably go into the navy and maybe see the world. Then I'll get married and that kind of thing. But, you know, it all takes time, so I can't hurry it along. You know what I mean?"

"Do you feel you're on the right path now?"

"I think so," Richie said. He looked into Dr. Talley's eyes, then away to the bookcase against the far wall. "I have to get a good

apart. One of them looked like me and Effie tearing each other apart. I didn't tell them what I had seen.

"Don't you think you need to go to school?"

It was too hard waiting to see if he was mad. Too hard waiting for him to come into the room as if he was somebody you could never know. That's what Effie said, that waiting for him was just terrible.

What I had to do was to stop eating his food and messing up his apartment and not bringing in a cent to pay for anything. I didn't have a job, so I went down to the navy recruiter and found out what I needed to do.

"Do you feel you're on the right path now?"

I stink, though.

What I had to do was get away from the bad person I had become and not let that plan. Organize my life better so I make the right moves and get on with my life."

"What do you mean exactly when you say get on with your life? Does it involve going back home? Going to school?"

"Yeah, I guess," Richie answered. "Whatever comes."

"Richie, in the best of all worlds, what will you be doing five years from now?" Dr. Talley asked. "Do you know what I mean when I say the best of all possible worlds?"

"Sure. What I'll probably do is be in the navy and maybe living in Seattle on a ship and then my folks will come out and see me and we'll have dinner right there on the ship. In the navy, anytime you get

be the real me. If I got into the navy and went away on a ship, I could wear a navy uniform and follow all the rules that the navy had. They had a book of rules, so you couldn't make a mistake and get into trouble. All you had to do was follow the rules and they would like you and then you would be all right. Effie called the house once when nobody was home but me and told me she was living in Seattle in her own apartment.

"Richie, in the best of all worlds, what will you be doing five years from now?" Dr. Talley asked. "Do you know what I mean when I say the best of all possible worlds?"

If I lived in Seattle and followed the rules of the navy, then he and my mother and Effie could come and see me and I would be big as anything, with all of my navy guys with something that big you call it a ship, you don't call it a boat. Then, after we have dinner, my mom and dad will go home and maybe I'll talk a bit to Effie and then she'll go home and then the ship will sail off. I know it's just a dream, but that's what I would like."

"You're a long way from that now," Dr. Talley said.

"I'm fifteen now," Richie said. "But I won't stay fifteen forever. You know, nobody stays fifteen forever. You get 365 days and you're another year older."

"Richie, our time is up today. I'll see you next week. I'd like you to think about why you're here, and why you left school. You think we can talk

me and we would all eat on the ship and the rules we would follow would be navy rules and we would all know them.

Then when we finished eating he and Mom would leave and on the way home they would talk and he would tell her how I was following all the rules and had got myself together. I don't know what he would say about Effie.

A shoe's a long way from a hat now. Yes.

That's what he said, too. He said I could never get away. But that's not true, because nobody stays fifteen forever.

The time is up, and Dr. Talley is talking like he thinks he can find the old Richie, the Richie that was always doing wrong things and needed the belt. He wants me to think about what happened and then say why I did the things I about it next time?"

"Yeah, sure," Richie said.

He stood, following Dr. Talley's lead.

In the hallway the attendant, a tall, black man with stooped shoulders was waiting.

"See you next week, Richie." Dr. Talley shook his hand and nodded toward the attendant.

The walls in the hallway were painted two colors, gray on the bottom and off-white on the top. Richie walked, head down, back to the C wing. He couldn't help smiling.

did, to say I wasn't wrong.

When he had the belt in his hand and was asking me why I did what I did, why I broke the cup, or why I didn't go to school or anything I did he would always tell me not to lie. "Don't lie to me, boy," he would say. "I can tell when you're lying."

But what he won't know, what nobody will know, is that who they see is not me. I'll be gone, but I'll send out my image, and he'll think it's me. The image will feel the same to him and look the same because he only knew the outside, anyway. It's funny to think about it. It really is.

A NOTE FROM WALTER DEAN MYERS

Books have always been friendly to me. When I was going to school in Harlem books were the secret friends I brought home. When I had speech difficulties, which I had most of my younger life, I could communicate with books. Writing poems, stories, and, eventually, books came naturally, the way hanging out with people who like you comes naturally.

I published first in the sixties while working days as a messenger. It was a wonderful feeling to be a published writer. There was a truth to it that was somehow more solid than the things I could touch and feel around me. I've been searching for repeats of that feeling, that truth, ever since.

Stories come from my life, from memories of things I've done or things I've imagined doing. Sometimes the aspects of stories are obvious. I was a foster child and so I often write about foster children. My brother died in Vietnam and so I wrote *Fallen Angels* about that war. I met my biological father when I was grown. That, too, became part of a story in *Somewhere in the Darkness*. "The Escape" is no different in this respect. In my teens I had a brief skirmish with the legal system. It seemed to me at the time that all the agencies involved, as well as the school, were against me. In a very real way I felt trapped by a system I thought I hadn't really offended. The details, of course, are made up of the material I keep in the Fiction Box under my bed.

The beast is in the labyrinth.

You see it most clearly, if you see it at all, on the dangerous threshold of dream. The candle has been blown out, or the wick snuffed; the night has snuggled in to lie with you in your blankets, the day with its particular difficult perfection recedes. Just before you sleep you may catch the thud of a hoof on stone, near, oh nearer than can be possible. The hot, meaty breath on your shoulder blade. Your limbs twitch; you start; you think someone has said your name. No one is there, and the no one is the Minotaur.

ATHLETE

BY GREGORY MAGUIRE

He makes for shore. From above, he is a dark bobbin cutting through the silk of the sea; there is only a head, turning regularly as he takes in air. Then, landfall. Heaving himself up on the sand. Athlete on the strand. Greek, but blond as Croesus's gold, now that the morning light sees more of him. He shakes out his hair and rests his hands on his knees, bent over for a minute, gasping. The water runs off his limbs and muscles; he is dry almost at once, but for his hair.

The word "athlete" serves better than the words "adolescent" or "teenager" or "young adult." Athlete, from the Greek, derived from *athlein,* to contend for a prize, derived more distantly from *athlon,* meaning both contest and prize. It is when you are young—when you are not yet old—that you struggle to win. That you enter the contest, find your footing against your opponent, set yourself against an adversary the better to know who you might yourself be. It is when you are young, also, that you are itself the prize, though the price of learning this is age.

He knots a cloth around his hips, not from modesty but to protect himself from the brambles that clutch the hillside. The island has risen out of the sea and given itself to the athlete; it has no problem providing the length of cloth. It would generate a sword and a shield for such a specimen of man, were it needed; but Theseus is young enough to be without that need yet. With head thrown back, he drinks in the air; the grumps in his muscles relax; he moves forward across the sand to the pebbly verge, and thence into the brush, up toward destiny.

Youth, being youth, has no past or future. Theseus has forgotten his earlier adventures. He has almost forgotten the six other young men who form part of the sacrificial offering sent annually to King Minos of Crete. They are behind in a ship he has slipped from; he sprang overboard not to escape his fate but to meet it earlier.

Legend says that the young victims are led into a maze and left there to wander, searching for an exit they never find. They die of starvation and broken hopes. Or, a worse fate, they are met by the Minotaur and devoured. *So glad you could drop by for dinner.* The Minotaur has not yet been deified by Renaissance painters or trivialized into a Disney cartoon character. Maybe the victims have seen a few scratches of white line on a black field, curving about the edge of an amphora—a creature with the limbs of an athlete and the head of a bull. Maybe they have recognized it.

The beast in the labyrinth.

You see it most clearly, if you see it at all, on the dangerous threshold of a dream. The candle has been blown out, or the wick snuffed; the night has snuggled in to lie with you in your blankets; the day with its particular difficult perfection recedes. Just before you sleep you may catch the thud of hoof on stone, near, oh nearer than can be possible. The hot, meaty breath on your shoulder blade. Your limbs twitch; you start; you think someone has said your name. No one is there, and the no one is the Minotaur.

It is as close as most of us come, but Theseus, bravest hero of sunrise Athens, comes nearer. Makes for the labyrinth, which stands in walls of stone and cruel impenetrable thicket on the fiercest brow of Crete, like a crown, like a granite headache, like a tombstone.

He pauses halfway, not to catch his breath but to look about. This is the world: acres of heaving turquoise fields sprouting white froth of blossoms, across whose impermanent furrows ride the ships of Attica. The sky above is crystalline and frangible, for every night stars puncture it and the gods reappear in their starry outlines. The islands of the Cyclades, footfalls of an older goddess, still tremble with her passing. The future is a thin line between the sky and the sea; it is called a horizon, and it is always there and never here.

Theseus catches sight of the boat moving into the harbor, the other six sacrificial victims drawing themselves to their fate, in strokes of oar that beat wrinkles of light into the water gone clear by the mirrored backing of the sandy floor just offshore. He turns again, and sees the maiden on the cliff. She is, she must always be, the daughter of the goddess, because she is as beautiful in her way as Theseus is in his.

She is also the daughter of the King, King Minos of Crete, at whose command these blood sports commence. She is Ariadne. If Theseus is sculpted—muscle and its rub of skin showing marble what to hunger to be if it cannot be mute and buried in the earth—then Ariadne is scalloped. She is a series of parallel abbreviations; the folds of her tunic caress the folds of her shoulders, her breasts, and her strong, soft limbs. She is drop-dead gorgeous, knockout time, no two ways about it, and stories about her can survive a lapse in elevated tone, for the thing that she is— arresting Beauty—endures once it is met, in much the same folds of the mind that also conceal the Minotaur.

Theseus draws nearer. She meets his level gaze with her own. The wind that will one day drive the ten thousand windmills in the valley of the same name now drives her hair about her face. She is dark where he is fair; she is coal and shadow of royal porphyry, he is gold and ivory. There is a sudden detonation, like a flare-up of a corona around the sun. The thing that happens there on that hill is only cheapened by the name of love, at least love in its modern dime-store sense. It is instead a different kind of sacrifice, a mutual amazement, a giving up and taking in. It is, in its way, a conquest and a prize both, for both of them. It is religion without past or future. Ariadne unbound; Theseus with both hands gripping the horizon before him.

To save him from the beast, she hands him a ball of thread. Why the thread? Why airy muscle of flax spun into a line as thin as a horizon? Thread is the thing that you cannot drag across the sea, from horizon to horizon, to learn your way back; it is the early form of the breadcrumbs that Hansel and Gretel drop to learn their way back. Theseus kisses Ariadne, and she kisses him, and the ball of string passes from her hand to his.

The other youths are now landed on the beach, and beginning to find their path up the hillside. Theseus is to save them, and himself, and all future victims of the beast. He is to do it soon, before his companions meet up with Ariadne and claim her for their own, or she them. He would not put it past them, nor blame her, but he cannot wait for it to happen. He must go forward and meet his fate, and change theirs.

The labyrinth. A gate of groaning iron on dark hammered hinges. It opens with a sucking sound, a throb as of the ventricle of an organ, the tightened ring of a muscle, and Theseus with his sword in hand—there has come a sword to hand, as there will, unbidden—passes through. Twisting corridors, branching alleys. Everywhere, a grandeur of dusk. The stench of the dead. The rot. The dust. The coldness—here and there, ellipses of snow run up into the corners of dead ends, where even light has been trapped, and so expired. The dark, of course, a kind of dark that lives within the atoms of light, light's dark core. The sound as of seashells, the wind in the stony volutes of the maze, twisting airy atonal chords. Here is a knucklebone, half chewed. Here, a scrap of white linen with gold embroidery, the key design, locking in regular steps just to where the fabric is ripped, and edged with the black of dried blood.

The cord unwinds as Theseus proceeds. He winds it back up when he finds a cul-de-sac. He moves ahead by instinct, not logic. There is an easy solution to mazes: Always keep to the left. Or is it the right? This solution, however, presumes the universe is built on a certain design, and that presumption has not yet arisen in the world. And instinct works better than logic for the athlete.

There is the sound of—

Or what is it?

Hoofbeats like heartbeats, like the beat of the wings of carrion crows, rotating nearer, dissolving away.

The light begins to ebb in distinctive pulses like an oil lamp flickering through its last lick of fuel. Theseus wades through runnels of dark as he waded that last bit of sea, coming naked onto the beach. He is naked now but for his sword and the ball of string.

And an odor of boiling marrow in a corroding iron cauldron . . .

And the fear dries the last of the ocean's damp from his brow, and his hair is now gold leaf, flamed with the force of his intention.

And the grunt, nearby, of a darker intention, and a sound that is a hybrid—part chuckle, part groan—a hybrid as the Minotaur is a hybrid, part man, part bull.

And the last corner turned, and the string run out, and the Minotaur there in the dark.

Moving up nearer. Snuggling in to lie in your blankets, to lay its hot breath on your shoulder blade, to snort just beyond your peripheral vision, and to disappear when you turn to see, when, up on your elbows, you start to consciousness.

But Theseus is athlete. He is both contest and prize. And the Minotaur needs to be killed, or Theseus will never be able to take the story out of the maze; and then we will never know, precisely, what it is that groans at us from the corner of our sleep.

The beast makes its rush.

Whose heart is beating so loud?

The sword flashes in the gloom. The roar is cut down in separate, stuttering syllables. The rage of tempest breath is reworked into glottal gasps. The muscle relaxes. The backbone arches first back, then forward. The bull's head throbs, and nods, and the horns that are nearly talons, nearly ring-round like manacles, make a musical sound as they strike against the floor of the labyrinth.

There is a death in the chamber, death with its own particular perfection. But Theseus has not lost his string, so he cannot lose his way. Ariadne waits. The Minotaur is over.

But the snow in the corner is melting, and the light is returning, and the light falls onto the pool of water, onto the smallest slice of inland sea caught there in a hollow in the floor, and a trick of the light catches his eye, and he waits and kneels to look. He should not kneel, he should not look, but, in a way, there is no choice.

The pool at the center of the labyrinth is not just melted snow, he sees; it is ringed with thick strings of the blood of the beast. It is a pattern of maze, the dark and the light, the red viscous opacity and the clear silvery threads, ineluctably entwined. He cannot see himself through the red, but in the silver he sees his reflection, in narrow crescents and wheels, and he kneels to look. Kneels, and feels the ache in a muscle in his back; kneels, and takes a steadying hold on his sword, for balance.

The golden crown of hair falls across his brow, and he can make out the stump of a knob, and another: the start of bull's horns. The sob that escapes is the kind of bellow that only those without language can make.

A NOTE FROM GREGORY MAGUIRE

A little about me, and a little about this story.

I was born and raised in upstate New York, but I've lived most of my adult life in Massachusetts and England. I've taught college and middle school, and I speak as a visiting author all over the country; mostly, however, I'm a writer. My most recent books? For adults, *Wicked*, the life story of the Wicked Witch of the West from *The Wizard of Oz*. For younger readers, *Oasis* and *Missing Sisters*, as well as a new comic series called The Hamlet Chronicles, which began with *Seven Spiders Spinning* and continues with *Six Haunted Hairdos*. Watch out soon for *Five Alien Elves*!

Now about the birth of this story, "Athlete."

During an advanced credit English seminar I took in middle school, I came across the A. E. Housman poem called "To an Athlete Dying Young," with its memorable image of youth and death: "The time you won your town the race / We chaired you through the marketplace. . . . Today, the road all runners come, / Shoulder-high we bring you home. . . ." I remember realizing that the death of the athlete wasn't necessarily the grave, but—perhaps more painful—was instead the age that he had to live beyond his youthful prowess and beauty and talent. It's a similar story to that of Snow White's stepmother, who studies the mirror vainly for proof she is still the fairest in the land. In some ways, of course, growing up means being liberated, but there are a few ways in which it doesn't mean that at all.

Recently I read Roberto Calasso's remarkable study of Greek myths called *The Marriage of Cadmus and Harmony.* (I had read Edith Hamilton's *Mythology* the same summer I first encountered the Housman poem.) Readers well versed in Greek myths may take exception to my trick ending—there is no version of the story of Theseus and the Minotaur in which Theseus's victory is so cruelly twisted into entrapment. But Calasso's central point is that mythology can support contradictory tellings of the same tale; indeed, this is the essence of mythology. I was convinced by his argument. It's in that spirit that "Athlete" came to me.

I was falling down a dark, disorderly tunnel. There was no end in sight. Coffee grounds were in my eyebrows, my hands smelled like used tea bags. I was exhausted, syrup encrusted, I'd had to go to the bathroom for three hours. People were going to get their own coffee—the ultimate defeat for any waitress. I looked at my haggard reflection in the coffee urn. My only consolation was that I wouldn't live until noon.

PANCAKES

BY JOAN BAUER

The last thing I wanted to see taped to my bathroom mirror at five-thirty in the morning was a newspaper article entitled "Are You a Perfectionist?" But there it was, courtesy of my mother, Ms. Subtlety herself. I was instantly irritated because Allen Feinman had accused me of perfectionism when he broke up with me last month. The term he used was "rabid perfectionism," which I felt was a bit much—but then Allen Feinman had no grip on reality whatsoever. He was rabidly unaware, if the truth be known, like a benign space creature visiting Earth with no interest in going native. I tore the article off the mirror; this left tape smudges. Dirty mirrors drove me crazy. I grabbed the bottle of Windex from the closet and cleaned off the gook until the mirror shined, freed of yellow journalism.

I glowered at the six telltale perfectionist signs in the now crumpled article.

(1) Do you have a driving need to control your environment?
(2) Do you have a driving need to control the environment of others?

(3) Are you miserable when things are out of place?

(4) Are your expectations of yourself and others rarely met?

(5) Do you believe if something is to be done right, only you are the one to do it?

(6) Do you often worry about your performance when it is less than perfect?

Number six had particular sting, for it was that very thing that Allen Feinman had accused me of the day he asked for his green and black lumberjack shirt back, a truly spectacular shirt that looked a lot more spectacular on me than it did on him because it brought out the intensity of my short black hair and my mysterious brown eyes. He had accused me of numbers one through five as well, but on this last fateful day he said, "The problem with you, Jill, is that if the least little thing goes wrong, you can't handle it. Everything has to follow this impossible path to perfection. Someday, and I hope it's soon for your sake, you're going to have to settle for sub-par performance and realize that you're imperfect like the rest of us." He stormed off like an angry prophet who had just delivered a curse, muttering that if I was like this at seventeen, imagine what I would be like at thirty.

"Good riddance," I shouted. "I hope you find a messy, inconsiderate girlfriend who can never find her purse or her car keys, who has no sense of time, no aptitude for *planning*, and that you spend the rest of your adolescent years on your hands and knees looking for your contacts!"

I padded down the hall to my bedroom. It was Sunday morning. I was due at my waitress job at the Ye Olde Pancake House in forty-five minutes. I sat on my white down quilt, saw the chocolate smudge, quick got up and brushed the smudge with my spot remover kit that I kept in my top dresser drawer, being careful to brush the nap against the grain. I put the kit back in the drawer, refluffed my two white pillows, plucked a dead leaf off my philodendron plant, and remembered my second to last fight with Allen when he went completely ballistic at my selfless offer to alphabetize his CD collection with a color-coded cross-reference guide by subject, title, and artist.

Males.

I put on my Ye Olde Pancake House waitress uniform that I had ironed and starched the night before: blue, long-sleeved ankle-length dress, white apron, white-and-blue-flowered bonnet. I could have done without the bonnet, but when you're going for the ye olde look, you have to sacrifice style. I was lucky to have this job. I got it one week after my parents and I moved to town, got hired *because* I am a person of order who knows there is a right way and a wrong way to do things. I replaced a waitress who was a complete disorganized slob. As Howard Halloran, the owner of the Ye Olde Pancake House, said to me, "Jill, if you're half as organized and competent as you look, I will die happy." I smoothed back my short clipped hair, flicked a sesame seed off my just-manicured nail, and told him that I was.

"I have a system for everything," I assured him. "Menu first, bring water when you come back to take the order, call it in, bring coffee immediately to follow. Don't ever let customers wait." Then I mentioned my keen knack for alphabetizing condiments, which was always a bonus, particularly when things got busy, and how a restaurant storage closet should be properly organized to take full advantage of the space.

"You're hired," Howard Halloran said reverently, and put me in charge of opening and setting up the restaurant on Saturday and Sunday mornings, which is when nine-tenths of all pancakes in the universe are consumed and you don't want some systemless person at the helm. You want a waitress of grit with a strategic battle plan that never wavers. Sunday morning in a pancake house is war.

I tied my white apron in a perfect bow across my back, tiptoed past my parents' bedroom, taking care not to wake them, even though my mother had taken an insensitive potshot at me without provocation.

It's not like my life had been all that perfect.

Did I ask to move three times in eighteen months because my father kept getting transferred? Did I ask to attend three high schools since sophomore year? Did I complain about being unfairly uprooted?

Well . . . I did complain a little. . . .

Didn't I figure out a way to handle the pressure? When my very roots were being yanked from familiar soil, I became orderly and organized. I did things in the new towns so that people would like me and want to hire me, would want to be my friends. I baked world-class cookies for high school bake sales, even if it meant staying up till three A.M.; I joined clubs and volunteered for the grunge jobs that no one wanted; I always turned in a spectacular performance and people counted on me to do it. I made everything look easy. People looked up to me, or down, depending—I'm five four. And I sure didn't feel like defending all that success before dawn!

I tiptoed out the back door to my white Toyota (ancient, yet spotless) and headed for work.

Syrup, I tried explaining to Hugo, the busboy, must be poured slowly from the huge cans into the plastic pourers on the tables because if you pour it fast, you can't control the flow and you get syrup everywhere, which never really cleans up. It leaves a sticky residue that always comes back to haunt you. Syrup, I told him, is our enemy, but like Allen Feinman, Hugo was a male without vision. He couldn't anticipate disaster, couldn't cope with forethought and prevention; he let life rule him rather than the other way around, which was why *I* personally filled the syrup containers on Sunday mornings—maple, strawberry, boy-senberry, and pecan.

I had just filled the last containers and was putting them on the tables in horizontal rows. I had lined up the juice glasses and coffee mugs for optimal efficiency, which some people who shall remain nameless would call perfectionism, but when the place gets busy, trust me, you want everything at your fingertips or you'll lose control. I never lose control. Hugo had set the back tables and I followed him, straightening the silverware. You'd think he'd been born in a barn. Andy Pappas, the cook, was making the special hash browns with onion and green pepper that people loved.

I steeled myself for the hungry Sunday morning mob that would descend in two hours. I always mentally prepared for situations that I knew were going to be stressful—it helped me handle them right. I could see me, Shirl, and Lucy, the other waitresses, serving the crowd, handling the cash register. Usually Howard Halloran took the money, but he was taking a long-needed weekend off since his wife said if he didn't she would sell the place out from under him. I could see myself watching my station like a hawk, keeping the coffee brewing, getting the pancakes delivered hot to the tables. Do it fast, do it right—that was my specialty.

It was seven o'clock. Shirl and Lucy were late, but I knew that Lucy's baby was sick and Shirl was picking her up, so I didn't worry. They'd been late before. I myself was never late. I unlocked the front door, and a few customers came straggling in with their Sunday newspapers, settling in the booths. Nothing I couldn't handle. Things didn't start getting crazy until around eight-thirty. I had my system.

I took orders, walked quickly to the kitchen window. "Four over easy on eight with sausage," I said crisply. "Side of cakes." That was restaurant-speak for four plates of two eggs over easy with sausage and pancakes on the side. Andy tossed his spatula in the air, went to work. The man had total focus. He could have two dozen eggs cooking in front of him and he knew when to flip each one.

A young family came in with three small children; gave them the big table by the window. Got them kid seats, took their order.

"Number three."

That was my waitress number. Andy called the number over the loudspeaker when my order was ready and I went and picked it up. A nice time-efficient system. I walked quickly to the counter (running made the customers nervous), grabbed the eggs, sausage, and pancakes, carried them four up on my left arm to table six, smiled professionally. Everything all right here, folks? Everyone nodded happily and dug in. Everything was always merry and pleasant at the Ye Olde Pancake House. That's why people came. Merry people left big tips.

I checked the ye old wall clock. Seven forty-seven. Still no Shirl and Lucy. They'd never been this late. Allen Feinman had been more than an hour late plenty of times. Allen Feinman didn't care about time—his or anyone else's. I didn't understand the grave problems he had at first; I was so caught up in him—this cute, brainy, funny guy who really seemed to want a shot of discipline. I put in my usual extra effort into the relationship—baked his favorite cookies (cappuccino chip), packed romantic picnics (French bread, brie, and strawberries), thought about unusual things to do in Coldwater, Michigan, which was quite a challenge, but I went to the library and came up with a list of ten possible side trips around town that we could do for free.

"You're just so *organized*," he would say, which I thought was a true compliment. Later on, I realized, coming from him, it was the darkest insult.

Andy was flipping pancakes on the grill. I scanned my customers to make sure everyone was cared for, turned to dash into the bathroom quickly when a screech of tires sounded in the parking lot. I looked out the window. A lump caught in my throat.

A large tour bus pulled to a grinding halt.

I watched in horror as an army of round, middle-aged women stepped from the Peter Pan bus and headed toward the restaurant like hungry lionesses stalking prey.

It was natural selection—I was as good as dead.

"Number three."

I looked at Andy, who raised his face to heaven.

"Call them," I shrieked. "Call Shirl and Lucy! Tell them to get here!"

Andy reached for the phone.

I turned to the front door as the tour bus women

poured in. They were all wearing sweatshirts that read MICHIGAN WOMEN FOR A CLEANER ENVIRONMENT. "A table for sixty-six," said a woman, laughing.

My lungs collapsed. Sixty-six hungry environmentalists. I pointed to a stack of menus, remembering my personal Waitress Rule Number One: Never let a customer know you're out of control.

"Sit anywhere," I cooed. "I'll be right with you."

"If you wrote the menu on a blackboard you wouldn't waste paper," one said.

"Number three." I raced back to the kitchen. Pancakes for table eight. I layered the plates on my left arm, plopped butter balls from the ye olde butter urn on the pancakes. Andy said he'd tried Shirl and Lucy and no one answered. At least they were on their way. I raced to table eight. The little girl took one look at her chocolate chip pancakes and burst into tears.

"They're not the little ones," she sobbed.

"Oh, now, precious," said her father, "I'm sure this nice young lady doesn't want you to be disappointed."

I looked at the environmentalists who needed coffee. Life is tough, kid.

"Tell the waitress what you want, precious."

Precious looked at me, loving the control. She scrunched up her dimples, dabbed her tears, and said, "I want the teeny weeny ones, pwease."

"Teeny weeny ones coming up," I chirped, and raced

to Andy. "Chocolate silver dollars for the brat on eight," I snarled. "Make them perfect, or someone dies."

"You're very attractive when you get busy," Andy said laughing.

"Shut up."

The phone rang. I lunged for it. It was Lucy calling from the hospital. Her baby had a bronchial infection, needed medicine. She couldn't come in, but Shirl was on her way, she should be pulling onto the interstate now.

"Are you all right there, Jill?"

"Of course," I lied. "Take care of that baby. That's the most important thing."

"You're terrific," she said, and hung up.

I'm terrific, I told myself. I can handle this because, as a terrific person, I have an organized system that always works. I grabbed two coffee pots and raced to the tour group, smiling. Always smile. Poured coffee. They'd only get water if they asked. We're so glad you came to see us this morning. Yes, we have many tours pass through, usually we have more waitresses, though. It's a safe bet that any restaurant on this earth has more waitresses than the Ye Olde Pancake House does at this moment.

I took their orders like a shotgunner shooting clay pigeons.

Pull!

Pigs in a blanket.

Steak and fried eggs.

Buttermilk pancakes.

Betsy Ross (buttermilks with strawberry and blueberry compote).

Colonial Corn Cakes (Allen Feinman's favorite).

A round-faced woman looked at me, grinning. "Everything looks so good." She sighed. "What do you recommend?"

I recommend that you eat someplace else, ma'am, because I do not have time for this. I looked toward the front of the restaurant; six large men were waiting to be seated. Hugo was pouring syrup quickly into pourers to torture me, sloshing it everywhere. I said, "Everything's great here, ma'am. I'll give you a few seconds to decide." I turned to the woman in the next booth. The round-faced woman grabbed my arm. I don't like being touched by customers.

"Just a minute. Well . . . it all looks so good."

"Number three." I glared in Andy's direction. "And number three again."

A cook can make or break you.

The round-faced woman decided on buttermilk pancakes, a daring choice. I ran to the kitchen window. "Hit me," Andy said.

"I'd love to. You're only getting this once. Buttermilks on twelve. Pigs on four, Betsy's on three. Colonials on seven." I threw the rest of the orders at him.

"You have very small handwriting," he said. "That's often the sign of low self-esteem."

I put my hand down in one of Hugo's syrup spills, pushed back my bangs with it; felt syrup soak my scalp.

Andy said, "You're only one person, Jill."

I scanned the restaurant—juice glasses askew, hungry people waiting at dirty tables. I could do anything if I worked hard enough. Shirl would be here any minute.

"Waitress, we're out of syrup!" A man held his empty syrup container up. I looked under the counter for the extra maple syrup containers I had cleverly filled, started toward the man, tripped over an environmentalist's foot, which sent the syrup container flying, caught midair, but upside down by a trucker who watched dumbly as syrup oozed onto the floor in a great, sticky glop. I lunged for the syrup container, slid on the spill, felt sugared muck coat my exposed flesh.

"Hugo!" I screamed, pointing at the disaster. "Hot water!"

"Number three."

I moved in a daze as more and more people came. Got the tour bus groups fed and out. Had they mentioned separate checks, one woman asked?

Nooooooooo . . .

Made coffee. More coffee. Told everyone I was the only waitress here, if they were in a hurry, they might want to go someplace else. But no one left. They just kept coming, storming through the restaurant like Cossacks. People were grabbing my arm as I ran by.

"What's your name, babe?" asked a lecherous man.

"Miss," I snarled.

"Number three."

"I had a life when I woke up this morning! Everything was in place!"

Buckwheats on table three. The man looked at them like they were turds. He said, "You call these buckwheats? Buckwheats are supposed to be enormous and hearty." I'm the fall guy for everything that happens in the restaurant. It's my tip that's floating down the river waving bye-bye. I embraced my personal Waitress Rule Number Two: The customer is always right, even if they're dead wrong. I said, "That's the way we do them here, sir," and he said he can't eat them, he can't look at them, he'll have the buttermilks, not knowing the trouble he's caused me. Andy gets sensitive if someone sends the food back—he's an artist, can't handle criticism. You have to lie to him or he slows down. I raced back to the kitchen.

"The man's a degenerate," I said to Andy. "He wouldn't know a world-class buckwheat if it jumped in his lap. He doesn't deserve to be in the presence of your cooking."

The phone rang. I lunged for it. It's Shirl calling from someone's car phone on the interstate with impossible news. A Coca-Cola trailer truck had jackknifed, spilling cans of diet Coke everywhere. There was a five-mile backup. She'd be hours getting to work.

"Are you all right?" Shirl asked.

I looked at the line of cars pulling into the parking lot, the tables bulging with hungry customers, the coffee cups raised in anticipation of being filled, the line at the cash register. I heard a woman say how the restaurant had gone downhill, and the people were looking at me like I was their breakfast savior, like I had all power and knowing, like I could single-handedly make sure they were happy and fed. And I was ashamed that I couldn't do it, but no one could.

Not even me!

I tore off my ye olde bonnet. "I'm trapped in a pancake house!" I shrieked into the phone, and, like in all sci-fi stories, the connection went dead.

"Number three."

I limped toward him, a shadow of my former self.

"We're out of sausage," Andy said solemnly.

"Good. It's one less thing to carry." I stood on the counter, put my head back, and screamed, "We're out of sausage and it's not my fault!"

A man at a back table hollered that he needed ketchup for his eggs. I reached down in the K section under the counter. Nothing under K. I got on my knees, hands shaking, rifling through jams, jellies, lingonberries. *Hugo!* I shrieked.

He ran up to me.

"Ketchup, Hugo! Wake up! The sky is falling!"

He pointed to the C section. "Catsup," he said meekly.

I was falling down a dark, disorderly tunnel. There was no end in sight. Coffee grounds were in my eyebrows, my hands smelled like used tea bags. I was exhausted, syrup encrusted, I'd had to go to the bathroom for three hours. People were going to get their own coffee—the ultimate defeat for any waitress. I looked at my haggard reflection in the coffee urn. The only consolation was that I wouldn't live till noon.

"Waitress!"

I raced down the aisle to table twelve, seeing the hunted look in my customer's eyes. I wanted to be perfect for every one of you. I wanted you all to like me. I'm sorry I'm not better, not faster. Please don't hate me, I'm only one person, not even a particularly tall person.

"I'm sorry," I said to a table of eight, "but I simply can't do everything!"

I felt a ripple of crass laughter in the air. I turned. Allen Feinman had walked in with his parents.

No, God. Anything but this.

Our eyes met. I could hear the taunts at school, the never-ending retelling of this, my ultimate nightmare.

"Can I help, Jill?" He rolled up his shirtsleeves. Allen Feinman was offering to help.

I grabbed his arm. "Can you work the register?"

"Of course." Allen organized the people into a line, made change, smiled. He had such a nice smile. Thanked everyone for their patience, got names on lists.

Mrs. Feinman took off her jacket and asked, "Can I make coffee, dear?"

"Mrs. Feinman, you don't have to—"

"We've always been so fond of you, Jill."

I slapped a bag of decaf in her sainted hands. Mr. Feinman poured himself a cup of coffee and went back to wait in the car.

We whipped that place into shape. All I needed was a little backup. My pockets were bulging with tips, and when Shirl raced in at eleven forty-five, I pushed a little girl aside who'd been waiting patiently by the bathroom door and I lunged toward the toilet stall. Life is tough, kid.

By one-thirty the crowds had cleared. Lucy called—her baby was home and doing better. Allen Feinman and I were sitting at a back table eating pancakes. He said he'd missed me. I said I'd missed him, too. Hugo was speed-pouring boysenberry syrup, spilling everywhere—but somehow it didn't matter anymore. It was good enough.

And that, I realized happily, was fine by me.

A NOTE FROM JOAN BAUER

One of my earliest and most sustaining memories is of my grandmother telling me stories when I was a child. She was a professional storyteller with a great comic sense. More than any other person, she influenced my writing style and my approach to humor. She always wove humor into her stories, bridging the seriousness of life with the absurdity. That's what I try to do in my work. I need to laugh. Laughter is like oxygen to me.

I wanted to be a comedienne when I was younger. I grew up outside of Chicago in River Forest, Illinois, with definite plans for achieving greatness. I took various career paths to get there, among them, sales, marketing, advertising, and "food and beverage administrator," more commonly known as *waitress*. The genesis of "Pancakes" came from deep within. When I was in high school I worked at the local IHOP and actually spent a few hideous hours one Sunday morning without any backup. Unlike Jill in the story, I never got a boyfriend out of the experience, but I remember the sheer terror of dozens of hungry people looking to me and me alone for breakfast. To this day, whenever I walk into a pancake house, I hyperventilate.

My books for young adults include: *Squashed*, winner of the Delacorte Press Prize for a First Young Adult Novel and a *School Library Journal* Best Book of the Year; and *Thwonk*, an ALA Best Book for Young Adults.

My new YA novel, *Rules of the Road*, will be published by Putnam. It's the funny and poignant story of a high school girl, the shoe business, and how she overcomes a family legacy of pain and adversity. I've also written *Sticks*, a novel for middle readers about pool, math, and desperate science. I live in Connecticut with my husband, daughter, and dapper dog.

Voice of Omar: *Come with me. Let's fly, Kwame. Above our bodies.*

Voice of Kwame: *What? You ill?*

Voice of Omar: *I'm feeling lighter by the minute. Freer. Aw, man! Trip with me. Let's soar.*

Voice of Kwame: *Not me. I'm staying planted.*

Voice of Omar: *(joyful) Kwame! A brother can fly like a bird can't. A brother can get high. Above the pain. Above the pain, Kwame!*

CROSS OVER

BY RITA WILLIAMS-GARCIA

VOICE OF KWAME
VOICE OF OMAR
KID 1
KID 2
LADY
OTHER LADY
GIRL
EMS WORKERS

That was how fast it happened. BAT-TAT-TAT! followed by the screech of tires tearing down Second Avenue. There are no witnesses to the shooting. Only the bright marquee of the NuArt Cinema offering a misspelled invitation to check out the film. Next to the theater stands The Shing On Dragon, a Chinese take-out place. Off and on, The Shing On Dragon breathes neon fire on OMAR *and* KWAME, *who are both seventeen, both lying somewhere between Second Avenue, The Here and Now and What's Next. They face each other.*

VOICE OF KWAME: *(disgust)* Close your eyes.

VOICE OF OMAR: Huh?

VOICE OF KWAME: Your eyes, man. It's disgusting to see that. Aw man. . . . close 'em, will you?

VOICE OF OMAR: My eyes? What about your mouth?

VOICE OF KWAME: My mouth?

VOICE OF OMAR: Blood and teeth . . . foul!

VOICE OF KWAME: Nothing wrong with my mouth. I don't even taste the blood. But for real, Omar, close your eyes or wipe 'em. Just look at that blood. . . .

A crowd gathers around KWAME *and* OMAR, *then disperses. Only* KID 1, KID 2, *both about nine, and a* LADY *stand on the sidewalk looking down at* KWAME *and* OMAR, *who lie in the gutter.*

KID 1: Saw the whole thang A shoot-out! *(to* LADY*)* Say, this gonna be on TV?

LADY: Do I look like *Eyewitness News?*

KID 2: Then I didn't see nothing.

VOICE OF KWAME: Did you see it?

VOICE OF OMAR: Did you?

VOICE OF KWAME: All I remember . . . we were watching a flick . . some flick I ain't get . . .

VOICE OF OMAR: Credits rolled . . .

VOICE OF KWAME: That wacky music *(mimics a bebop sax solo)* or something like that.

VOICE OF OMAR: Stepped outside . . .

VOICE OF KWAME: And pad-dad-DOW!

VOICE OF OMAR: Not even that.

VOICE OF KWAME: Just PAT—

VOICE OF OMAR: *(pause)* Get up.

VOICE OF KWAME: *You* get up.

VOICE OF OMAR: Stuck?

VOICE OF KWAME: Like a mother.

OTHER LADY *joins the three onlookers.*

OTHER LADY: It was just a matter of time.

LADY: Umhm.

OTHER LADY: Too quiet up in here.

LADY: Quiet and peaceful.

OTHER LADY: Gang wars spreading like cancer.

LADY: Sure it's the gang wars?

OTHER LADY: Them knucklehaids shootin' up the parkway. Only a matter of time before they brought it down this way.

KID 1: Un-unh! Ain't no ganging up in here.

OTHER LADY: *(points finger at KID 1)* Did anyone ask your opinion?

KID 1: If they gang bangers, why ain't they got colors?

KID 2: Yeah. They sposed to have colors.

KID 1: On they haids.

KID 2: Dat's right! *(to* OTHER LADY*)* Like "Ain't *yo* mama on the pancake box?"

OTHER LADY: Well! See if I give a care when it's your little rail bones lying all shot up *(storms off).*

KID 1: *(To* KID 2*)* No. Ain't *yo* mama on the pancake box.

KID 2: Yo mama. *(*KID 2 *tags* KID 1, *who chases him around the bodies. They exit the scene running.)*

LADY: *(looking down at* OMAR *and* KWAME*)* Tell the truth, I think those two boys just here for the show.

VOICE OF KWAME: That's right. A flick I ain't get. Damn.

LADY: I think they the only ones went to see that movie. Some kind of new art. *(sighs)* Now that's a crime and a shame.

VOICE OF KWAME: Hear that? Hear that? Why I gotta follow yo ass?

VOICE OF OMAR: Follow me?

VOICE OF KWAME: You said, 'Let's get off the block. Can't expand your horizons on the same block, day in, day out. Remember that? *(beat)* I ain't even want to come out on a night like this. Coulda been watching TV. That's how it always goes. 'Kwame, let's check out this, check out that.' I'm always following. Seventh grade. You said, 'Let's get down with The Nation.' I said 'Cool.' Didn't know I had to give up the pork chop! Shoulda known when you said, 'Let's check out the NuArt Cinema—throw our heads into some culture.' Where was my radar? Damn! I coulda been watching TV, smackin' on the pork chop. Why you gotta be reaching for the next level, taking me with you?

A faint green light is visible over OMAR.

VOICE OF OMAR: Because I can see him. Always could.

VOICE OF KWAME: See who?

VOICE OF OMAR: Milkman. Flying.

VOICE OF KWAME: Milkman. *(thoughtful pause)* Milk— from that book—Man? *That* Milkman?

VOICE OF OMAR: I'm going that way, Kwame. Come with me. Let's fly, Kwame. Above our bodies.

VOICE OF KWAME: What? You ill?

VOICE OF OMAR: I'm feeling lighter by the minute. Freer. Aw, maaan! Trip with me. Let's soar. Like Milkman.

VOICE OF KWAME: Not me. I'm staying planted.

VOICE OF OMAR: *(joyful)* Kwame! A brother can fly like a bird can't. A brother can get high. Above the pain. Above the pain, Kwame!

VOICE OF KWAME: A brother can snap. *(beat)* This ain't English class. This is asphalt. Sidewalk. You and me twisted up. Our blood running into the gutter.

VOICE OF OMAR: We can get up!

VOICE OF KWAME: Or stay put.

VOICE OF OMAR: Let's get off the block! Fly!

VOICE OF KWAME: I am NOT following this time. Not

when we got everything here. (KWAME *grunts. He struggles to lift his arms. It's futile.*) Just keep thinking Mom's sweet potato pie.

VOICE OF OMAR: I'm tasting the sweetness.

VOICE OF KWAME: A'ight, a'ight. I got one for you. Music! The boom. The beats. The funk. Where can you get *that* but planet Earth?

VOICE OF OMAR: In me.

VOICE OF KWAME: Hah! You ain't no musical talent!

VOICE OF OMAR: If you take off with me, you'll feel vibrations, like I'm feeling them.

VOICE OF KWAME: Check yourself . . . don't even sound like my man anymore . . .

KID 1: He moved! The pretzled bloody one. Dja see that?

KID 2: Dead bodies don't move.

VOICE OF KWAME: But we're not dead!

KID 1: *(points to* KWAME*)* Maybe he's not—

VOICE OF KWAME: That's right, that's right. Nine-one-one. Did anybody call nine-one-one?

KID 2: Let's poke him with a stick.

LADY: Yawl stay back.

KID 1: A sharp stick.

KID 2: Get the stick! Get the stick!

LADY: You hear what I said? Don't mess with the dead.

KID 1: What if they ain't dead?

VOICE OF KWAME: *(hopeful)* That's right!

KID 2: *(excited)* He moved! Dja see it?

LADY: Get back now! Get back. They might not be dead . . . Might be in the spirit. Trying to cross over.

KID 1: Trapped?

The cooks and the owner of the Shing On Dragon come outside. The owner hands out menus to the onlookers while the cooks beat metal pots around KWAME and OMAR.

VOICE OF KWAME: STOP THE RACKET!!!

VOICE OF OMAR: *(laughs)*

VOICE OF KWAME: Ain't funny. They killin my ears.

VOICE OF OMAR: *(laughs harder)*

VOICE OF KWAME: What?

VOICE OF OMAR: We're already killed.

VOICE OF KWAME: Speak for yourself. You the one flying. I'm fighting to the end.

VOICE OF OMAR: *(as if reading a story)* The End.

VOICE OF KWAME: F*ck you, a'ight. Cause I ain't going out like this. Cut down for no reason by no body. Ain't did shit to no one. Ain't got on boat, sailed to Okinawa or wherever marines go. Ain't put out no fires, made no serious money, got with Shakirah, drove no car—new or old, wore no suit, sat buck naked in my own crib, watched the Knicks take it all, or ate me a philly steak with extra sloppy cheese. *(cries)* Not even the cheese, man. The extra sloppy . . . *(sobs)* Naw, man . . . catch the dead-eye shuttle on out if you want to, but I ain't flying with you. I ain't going out like a sucker.

A GIRL *walks by.*

VOICE OF KWAME: Did she see us, man?

VOICE OF OMAR: *(mystically)* See . . .

VOICE OF KWAME: That girl. She could know us. I don't want no one seein' us like this. *(beat)* My mouth. How bad does it really look?

VOICE OF OMAR: The body, Kwame. Give up the body . . .

VOICE OF KWAME: You know what's your problem?

VOICE OF OMAR: I'm floating above problems . . . above my body . . .

VOICE OF KWAME: You ain't got love in your heart. Right here, beatin strong. You wouldn't toss your life away, *poof!* if you had someone holdin' on.

VOICE OF OMAR: Holding on?

VOICE OF KWAME: My sisters got love for me. I got two sisters—twice the love. My mother got love for me. Pops, too. Who knows? Maybe Shakirah could be loving me. Who knows? Question is, who got love for you?

VOICE OF OMAR: All the love I have felt, I am at this moment. Now hold on to that!

VOICE OF KWAME: There you go, expanding. Reaching for the next level. Just remember this. Reaching got us lying shot up on the curb. NuArt *(grumbling)* Cinema . . .

Wailing sirens and flashing red lights flood the scene.

KID 1: E-M-S! E-M-S!

KID 2: *(with fake gun)* Make a move and I'll shoot.

KID 1: That's the police, not the E-M-S, E-M-S!

LADY: Lotta good it does now.

VOICE OF KWAME: Hear that? Hear that? We saved! We saved, man! Marines! Here I come! Okinawa, here I come! Shakiraaaah! Get me a philly steak with the extra sloppy cheese! *(pause)* Think they'll clean us up first?

EMS WORKERS *push the crowd out of the way. They look at* OMAR, *then at* KWAME. *They kneel over* KWAME *performing what appears to be brutal life-saving measures.* KWAME *moans in pain.*

VOICE OF OMAR: Let go.

VOICE OF KWAME: Shit hurts. *(gasps)* They pounding my chest.

VOICE OF OMAR: Let go, man. There's peace . . .

VOICE OF KWAME: When I get up, I'm gonna *(coughing)* round those suckers.

VOICE OF OMAR: Give up, give up, give up the—

VOICE OF KWAME: NO!

VOICE OF OMAR: Free yourself.

VOICE OF KWAME: Aaaagh! It hurts, I ain't lying! Awww, man, it hurts! What they doin to me?

VOICE OF OMAR: Just let go. You and me, Kwame. Let's trip to the next level . . .

VOICE OF KWAME: Tubes! Tubes! I feel them. Down my nose, down in my gut.

VOICE OF OMAR: Follow the light . . .

VOICE OF KWAME: *(choking and gasping)*

Gradually OMAR *is overcome by light.*

VOICE OF OMAR: Fly . . .

VOICE OF KWAME: I can't hear you! Where you at? Omar?

EMS WORKER: We got a live one!

VOICE OF KWAME: Can't hear you! Omar . . .

VOICE OF OMAR: Peace.

A NOTE FROM RITA WILLIAMS-GARCIA

So what's that about? Did I really see two guys shot up on the sidewalk? Did it really happen?

The truth is, "Cross Over" takes place where all my stories take place—in my restless imagination. I am your classic daydreamer, taking images to places where they can run rampant. If you peeked in my mind while I was dreaming up this story you'd see the final scene between Milkman and Guitar in Toni Morrison's *Song of Solomon*, images from Walt Whitman's earthy and surreal poems, and an abandoned movie theater with a tombstone of a marquee. You'd hear a loud pop that could have very well been a gunshot followed by the sounds of tires tearing down the street.

I had "Cross Over" in my head two years ago, but every time I sat down to write, the pen would completely miss the pad. I just couldn't get it going. I had all my images, characters, things they'd say, things that would happen—down to the last word! It didn't matter. Nothing I wrote looked right or sounded right, so I put it away. Besides, I had to concentrate on school. (I was in my last year of my master's degree program.) It was there, in my postmodern drama class, reading all of those far-out plays, that I realized my story was trapped in a story format when it needed to be a play. And here it is!

I've always been a writer, a daydreamer, a dancer, a geek. My writing career began as a kid, telling lies, typing them up, and sending them to magazines. I got loads of rejection letters but I figured, if Hemingway could do it, so could I. I finally sold my first story at fourteen to *Highlights for Children*. I then sold a story to *Essence* magazine while in college, and wrote the first draft of my novel *Blue Tights* before graduating. Years later *Blue Tights* was published by Lodestar Books, and things started happening. I then wrote *Fast Talk on a Slow Track*, followed by *Like Sisters on the Homefront* for Lodestar. My latest novel is titled *Every time . . . A Rainbow Dies*.

When I'm not writing, I work full time for a marketing company as their software distribution and production manager. I'm married and have two daughters, Michelle and Stephanie, who also daydream.

Me and Thommo, we was only nineteen. Only kids, see? But they made us go. Put us down in the sewers. Tunnel rats, that's what they called us. Tunnel rats. Spent our time under the ground. Under the war, see? Checking for enemy snipers that hid down there. The Viet Cong raiders beneath the city. In the drains, like. In the sewers. Like another world it was. There was this pretty little white snake lived down there. Lived its whole life in the dark. Pure white it was. Silvery. "Two-Step," we called it. If it bit you, you'd take two steps and you'd be gone . . .

TUNNEL RAT DREAMING

BY GARY CREW

The lone Sopwith biplane dropped from the clouds that capped the night sky. "I see you," the pilot muttered as a silvered Zeppelin cut the searchlight's sweeping beam. "I see you . . ." and his hand reached for the trigger, twin wing-cannon at the ready. Ready to spit fiery death.

A licky-wet tongue shattered Jimmy's dream of glory. He groaned and sat up. There was Max beside his bed, dog tags tinkling, begging for a walk.

"Okay," Jimmy whispered. "Okay." Just let me get dressed. And don't go waking up Mom and Dad. It's Sunday, Okay?"

The early morning sun was weak; the faded blue of the sky cloud streaked. A raw wind from the docks cut Jimmy's face, pinking his cheeks. He turned up the collar of his bomber jacket and tagged along behind Max.

Max was a good dog. Well trained. Obedient. He never needed a lead. He was always there, just off Jimmy's right wing . . . and for a block or two—maybe more—the

Sopwith pilot was back in his cabin, mustache twitching, his thumb pressuring the cannon trigger.

The fighter powered into a dive, its sluggish target caught in the cross-beams of the searchlights' deadly glare.

"This is for my wife," the pilot spat, pressing the trigger home. "And my kids. You murdering . . ."

But Max suddenly bolted, snapping Jimmy into reality.

A rat. A huge dockside rat streaked away. Max was in pursuit.

Jimmy followed, cursing.

Down narrow lanes they ran—rat—dog—boy—as bins toppled, boxes tumbled, cans and bottles rolled and rattled until, at last, the rat slipped beneath a fence of wire and wood and the chase stopped dead.

Max whined as Jimmy grabbed him by the folds of skin at the back of his neck. But there was no holding the hunter. The dog broke away, dropped flat, spread-eagled on its gut, slithered under the fence, then took off again across a stretch of concrete to disappear in the shadow of a building: a huge, ramshackle building of crumbling brick. Jimmy clutched the wire and stared through.

Where were they? What was this place? Not a warehouse like the other dockside buildings. A warehouse didn't have chimneys. This place—whatever it was—had three. Four, counting the one that had fallen, that seemed to have snapped, halfway, like a broken column in a cemetery.

Lightning?

A bomb?

Jimmy walked on, searching for a gate. "Max!" He called. "Here, Maxy, here!" The dog did not return. Did not obey. The urge to hunt, to kill, was too strong.

Jimmy cursed under his breath. He wanted to get back to his snug, homey room. To his warm bed. To the Air Ace comics he'd bought the day before, and really wanted to finish . . . but then he saw a gate—or what was left of a gate—its hinges sagging so that it hung askew, leaving a gap.

Cautiously, Jimmy stepped through.

He crossed the cracked and lifting concrete of the car park and entered the shadow of the building. A chill crept into his bones. A chill of sudden fear. He didn't like this place. There was something about it. Something *bad*.

The looming walls of the building surrounded him on three sides. There was no sign of Max. He called again, but there was no response. Not a bark. Not a whimper. And yet, as he peered into the shadows, he could just make out a door—a door swinging open and shut, open and shut— in the cold sea wind. A door lead in to a deeper darkness beyond.

Jimmy mustered his fighter pilot's courage, crossed the yard, and peered in.

There was a corridor, dark and narrow, so he walked carefully, the tips of the fingers of his right hand brushing the rough brick walls, his left hand extended, like an antenna, in case there should be any lurking obstacle—any danger—concealed in the dark ahead.

He did not feel brave at all. No matter how hard he tried to remind himself—to remember his mission—the dream-courage of his comic book hero seemed to fade with the light.

The passage turned at right angles and a patch of early morning sunlight, falling from a grimy window far above, appeared ahead. He moved toward it and, by its pale light, he saw the entrance to a room—a huge, yawning room, like some sort of old workroom, or factory—littered with fly-wheels and motors and pulleys and conveyors and gauges and switches and coils of cable, but nothing seemed ordered; no crates or boxes of goods were stacked or labeled; no evidence of an actual *product*. . . unless all had been destroyed when the chimney fell. When the lightning struck. When the bomb went off . . .unless this was the work of vandals. Or sabotage . . .

But winding through the chaos was a pathway—a curious, snaking pathway of bare, gray concrete; white, almost silvery by that pale light. A path that lead toward another room, deeper yet, darker, at the heart of this awful place.

Jimmy did not want to go on. To go in. "Max," he called—his voice a little higher, a little shakier— "Maxy, come here. Now!"

As his words echoed and re-echoed from brick and glass and concrete, he heard the faintest sound. A pretty sound. Like bells. A distant tinkling, like tiny bells.

Max, he thought. Maxy's tags. But he did not call again, just to be certain that it *was* Max. Not something else . . . Stooping low to conceal himself among the machines, the piles of rubbish, he kept on.

He reached the end of the machine room and peered around a door. There, by the embers of a dying fire, he saw a man. Scruffy. Old. His huge hands stretched out, fingers up, palms toward the fire. His clothes were drab and filthy. A black woollen cap, filled with holes, was pulled down over his ears, over his forehead. And a long gray beard—a flowing river of a beard—covered his chest, his face, his mouth.

Jimmy gave up all pretense of courage. He backed away. He was getting out. Max could find his own way home. He had before. Plenty of times.

Just when he thought he had succeeded, Max bounded toward him barking, jumping, licking—crazy—until the boy fell back into rubbish, into the piles of iron and wood and glass that filled the place; and with the din of the dog's barking, the crash of rubbish falling, his cry of shock or fear was lost. When he'd pushed Max away and sat up, Jimmy saw that the man had not moved; that Max had trotted back to sit beside him, beside the fire, and the man was looking in his direction, his head turning slowly from side to side—like a snake, mesmerizing its prey before striking for the kill. But there was no hunter in the man's eyes. Only a dreamy sort of peace. And when he spoke, his voice was peaceful, too. Dreamy and slow and deep . .

"Thommo," he said. "Thom-mo. . . "

It seemed to the boy that this word came from the man's beard, rather than his mouth; came flowing out of that river of a beard, and for a second he thought that someone stood in the doorway behind him. Someone the man was talking to, or calling. Jimmy checked over his shoulder. No one was there. No looming shadow. Not a sound of a footfall. Jimmy looked back at the man. Max was squatting beside him, head down on his front paws, quite happy, dreaming into the fire. The boy edged forward, clicking his fingers for the dog to come. He was ignored. He moved closer, all the while ready to turn and run, his Spitfire courage long forgotten. He moved closer still, until he was almost beside the man, almost standing above him, and only then did the man speak again.

"I thought you were Thommo," he said, looking up so that Jimmy saw the paleness of his eyes. Tired looking. Worn out. But Jimmy's mouth was too dry to answer.

"Nice dog," the man said. "Your best friend, hey?"

"Yes," Jimmy muttered.

"I had a friend once," the man nodded, "but I lost him. In Nam. See? That's who I thought you was. My friend, see? Thommo . . . lost him, see?" As he spoke, his body began to rock backward and forward. "Lost my family, too . . ."

The boy realized then that this man was not looking into the fire, but beyond it, towards three rag dolls dangling from the rail of a conveyor, each suspended by a piece of string knotted beneath its arms. Three tattered dolls, dangling in air, their huge fabric eyes staring directly back at the rocking man.

"See? Don't you see?" the man said, speaking directly to them, "He will find me. Thommo will find me."

But the dolls did not respond—could not respond—and hung there, staring wide-eyed and silent, as if they were afraid.

"Mister . . ." Jimmy whispered, "Mister, are you okay?"

The man turned his head to look at him. In that moment his eyes were bright, alive, but it was no more than a flash of life from the fire, and passed again into faded blue. Into a vacant stare.

"Can I give you a hand?" Jimmy asked, his real self returning. His in-control self.

"I thought you was Thommo. I was waiting for Thommo."

"Thommo?" the boy repeated, looking around, still half expecting a person to appear from the shadows. "Who's Thommo?"

"A guy I went to school with. Then to Nam. Vietnam. Called up to fight, we were. Conscripted. Didn't know nothing about war. Didn't even know where that country was, see? In 1970, that was. Me and Thommo, we was only nineteen. Only kids, see? But they made us go. Put us down in the sewers. Tunnel rats, that's what they called us. Tunnel rats. Spent our time under the ground. Under the war, see? Checking for enemy snipers that hid down there. The Viet Cong raiders beneath the city. In the drains, like. In the sewers. Like another world it was. There was this pretty little white snake lived down there. Lived its whole life in the dark. Pure white it was. Silvery. "Two-Step," we called it. If it bit you, you'd take two steps and you'd be gone, see, poisoned. Drop dead. We done that duty for nearly two years, me and Thommo. Always together, see? Always a team . . ."

He looked away, back into the fir, his long, thin fingers gently fondling Max's throat.

"Was your friend Thommo supposed to meet you here?" the boy asked, even though it made no sense that anyone would want to meet a friend in this awful place.

But it made sense to the man, perfect sense, to his muddled, dreaming mind. "Sure he'll come," he said. "Sure he'll come. He'll find me. He has to, see?" And suddenly— causing the boy to start back, the man took his hand from Max's throat and reached to his own. "See? I got his tags. He'll be coming for them. To ask for them back, see? His identity. See?"

He bent his head and Jimmy saw two silver chains

around his neck. When he pulled them out from beneath his shirt, the boy saw that they had silver tags dangling from them. A jingling silver pair of tags. One on each chain. They were the same as Max's. The man lifted one chain over his head and held it out to Jimmy. "These are Thommo's tags," he said, placing the coiled chain in the boy's hand. "I kept them for him, see? Kept them safe. Waiting for him."

Jimmy nodded. This made some sense, at last, but . . . "So where is Thommo?" he asked. "How . . ."

The man turned back to the fire. His voice changed again to a rhythmic dreaming. His head rocked from side to side. He was remembering—imagining—and his singsong words fell like pictures from his mouth; the deep and flowing river of his beard.

"We was down in them sewers, see, the last time I saw Thommo. Safe, we were. Safe in the dark, right under ground. No 'two step' ever got us. And the war, the fighting and the killing and the noise of the bombs and fire and screams of the dying, well, that never got to us, either. We were safe down there, see? Down beneath the surface. Beneath the stone and concrete. But on our last day, on the day the Serge said we were getting out, going home . . ." He drifted off, lifting his head toward the dolls—his family, Jimmy imagined—then he sighed, and went on. "So we got out of them tunnels, see, pushed up the iron lid of this drain, this round iron cover, see, and in came the sky. This circle of sky. When we looked we saw this chopper was waiting for us. Hanging there, in that blue circle of sky, and this ladder hanging down, see, just above our heads. Just out of reach . . ." The man raised his arm, stretching out his filthy hands—his long, thin fingers—as if he were about to grab that ladder—that dreaming, imaginary ladder—so real in his mind.

"'You go first', Thommo said. 'You got family . . .' So I did. I grabbed that ladder and I hung on. When I made it up a couple of rungs, and was swinging free, in the air, like, I saw Thommo take hold and lift out, too. I thought that we were okay, see, since the chopper was climbing higher, real steady like, straight up. That was when I saw the city. The fires, the smoke, the dead lying all around. Soldiers—ours and the 'Cong's—civilians, kids . . . little kids all dead in the streets. In the gutters. In the piles of bricks and rubbish. Terrible it was. Terrible. But the chopper was getting me out. Taking me home. I was leaving all that behind, see, going back to my wife. My kids. Away from old "two step," away from . . .

"I looked down at Thommo, then, to see that he was okay, to give him a hand up like, but just as I did I heard shots. A rattle of rapid fire—I didn't see anything, like who did it—but Thommo was hit. Hit in the back. Shot in the back just as he was getting out. I saw him crumble, saw him look up to me, like he was asking for help—begging—then he started to slip. To let go, hand after hand, and fall back.

I grabbed for him, I did, true, but I was too late. I couldn't reach. Couldn't get a grip. But my fingers got his tags, see? Grabbed the chain round his neck, and when he fell, that chain was in my hand. Snapped off in my hand. But, Thommo, he was gone. Back into that pit. That dark. And that chopper, it didn't go back, see. Couldn't go back. Couldn't take the risk. And it just kept on lifting, see, kept on rising. Way up and out. Out of that place. That shooting and fire and smoke and death. Taking me home. Back home . . ."

It seemed to Jimmy that the man had forgotten he was there—that *anyone* was there—and he cleared his throat to let the man know. To remind him to go on. To tell what happened next. To Thommo.

But the man did not need reminding. He had stopped only to draw breath. And when he began again, with that same singsong deep river voice, the boy understood that this tale had been told many times. To many people—to *any* people—and now, to him, Jimmy, the would-be-if-he-could-be fighter pilot. The dreaming-bound-for-glory comic book fighter pilot. And with new understanding, Jimmy listened . . .

"When we got home there was nothing. No heroes' welcome. No brass band. No nothing. My wife and my kids were at the airport, sure, but after a couple of days she said to me—my wife, I mean— 'You need to get out. Get a job. Put all this war stuff out of your head. All this

Thommo stuff.' But I couldn't, see, I tried—I even went to doctors, see, I even took pills to get rid of it—to forget—but I couldn't. Then they started to call me crazy, see—tagged me—see—called me a looney. . . . Then my wife, she left me, see, and took my kids, because I wouldn't give up, see, I just couldn't. Because Thommo will come back. I know it. And I'll be waiting. Waiting in the dark. Like we used to. Someplace dark. That's where he'll find me. Or I'll find him. I reckon he'll come up behind me, out of the dark, see, in some tunnel, some subway, and when he does, he'll say 'Gotcha'—that was a game we played, see, like we was old two step sneaking out—striking out—and I'll say, 'Got you, boyo, . . . I got you . . .' and give him back his tags—see—his name . . . see? I'll give him back his . . . back his . . . his . . ."

There was no more to say. The man's head was still, the rhythmic nodding finished with the tale. When the boy crept forward to look, he saw that those pale and faded eyes were shut, the tale-teller lost in sleep.

And that was how Jimmy left him. He called to Max and left the place. But as he reached the entry to the tunnel, he stopped and looked back, whispering into the dark, "I'll be back, mister, I promise. I'll be back." Then he turned for home, following Max, as usual, who trotted on—nose down, tail high, tags jingling—into the dreamy peace of a bright, blue morning.

A NOTE FROM GARY CREW

The idea for my story "Tunnel Rat Dreaming" came to me in response to an item in Margaret Morton's photo-journalistic book, *The Tunnel,* which is an exposé of the lives of the homeless who live in a long disused railroad tunnel beneath New York. One of the characters interviewed was a "shell shocked" veteran of the Vietnam War. He told of how he had been a "tunnel rat" in Vietnam, scouring the maze of tunnels that the Viet Cong had burrowed to provide shelter from the fighting above while giving them easier access to surprise attack.

One of the most bizarre elements of the vet's story was his reference to the white snake that he called "Two Step," a reptile which lived in the dark tunnels, whose bite was so deadly that a soldier would walk only two steps before he died.

Another reason for my interest in the vet's story was that as a nineteen-year-old I was conscripted to fight in Vietnam myself. Being a pacifist, I refused to go and was taken to court. Those troubled times seem so long ago.

I now live with my wife in a cottage set among the wild and beautiful Blackall Ranges, near the sleepy country town of Maleny in the southeast corner of Queensland, Australia. I write mostly novels and short stories for teenagers, although my own three children are now adults. My adventures in writing have been quite wonderful and my books have gathered acclaim and prizes all over the world.

I am the author of *Strange Objects*, *No Such Country*, and *Angel's Gate*.

I sometimes think that maybe my life is too peaceful. It's so easy to spend a day sitting on my front porch daydreaming as lazy clouds drift over my blue and distant hills.

Carol wrenched her hand away from him and ran across the road. Without looking back she ran into the gardens. Steven ran after her. He was faster than she was and he caught up with her a few yards inside the gate.

"Don't run away from me, Carol. I just want to get to know you."

"I'm not sure I want to know you!"

AND STILL THE BIRDS KEEP CIRCLING

BY GILLIAN RUBINSTEIN

That's the boy," her mother said, making a birdlike gesture with her head toward the terrace. She glanced briefly, dartingly, then looked down at her half-empty coffee cup.

Carol looked at the boy. He was standing on the pavement, staring upward, hands in pockets, a blackish bomber jacket, leather maybe, jeans, hair neither short nor long, skin pale, not tanned, an unremarkable boy. She would never have looked twice at him. But her mother did. More than twice. She kept sneaking glances at him as if she were hungry for the sight of him, trying to pretend she wasn't.

"What boy?"

"He comes here a lot, I've seen him here often. He comes to watch the birds."

Carol watched her mother, watching the boy, watching the birds. She thought about the pattern they made, the connections between the three people and the birds, she herself so earthed and sensible, the birds soaring high and free and between them her mother and an unknown boy, tied together by something she hadn't yet grasped.

"Mum, I've got to go, I'll be late for afternoon school." The Grammar School, across the Botanical Gardens, suddenly seemed normal and almost desirable.

Her mother looked at her. Her dark eyes were huge and sorrowful, making her pale face look top heavy, like a nineteenth-century heroine, Jane Eyre or the woman in *The Piano*. Her face seemed to disappear below the eyes, as if in retreat from a life that was growing too difficult. The mouth was small and budlike, but tremulous and timid. The chin almost merged with the neck.

"We could go into town together, look at the shops."

"I can't, Mum. I've got to go to school!"

She knew she shouldn't have come. She never should have agreed to meet her mother for coffee in the lunch break between morning and afternoon school. Now she would be late, there would be explaining to do, and who could she tell, how could she explain, at the posh school where she was just a scholarship girl, that she was afraid her mother was going mad?

"He just watches the birds, all the time," her mother went on. "He comes ever so often, and watches the birds."

"Who is he?"

"Her mother gave her a strange look, almost sly, almost flirtatious. "What would you say if I told you he's your brother?"

It was another of her crazy fantasies. Carol felt like shaking her. She couldn't stand this confusion of reality and imagination in which people became long-lost relations, or threatening enemies. None of it was real except inside her mother's head.

"No, he's not," she said. She stood, picked up her schoolbag.

Her mother went on smiling, nodding her head infuriatingly, like a child with a secret. Her expression changed to one of apprehension when she saw Carol was really going.

"Can you pay, love?"

"What happened to the money you got out of the bank yesterday?" Carol felt dizzy. The gray world of the café, terrace, the arts center buildings tilted around her.

"I spent it."

"Where?" she said in fury.

"I had to buy something. Don't be cross, Carol, please, love. It's only money."

"Mum, I'm going to school. Get the tram and go home, okay? I'll see you after school."

Her mother dipped her spoon in the almost empty cup and scooped out the froth.

"Come on, I'll walk to the tram stop with you."

"Just let me finish my coffee," her mother replied. "No point wasting it."

"I've got to go!"

"I'll go home." Her mother nodded her head several times and smiled brightly.

"Promise?"

"I promise, Carol," she said obediently like a child.

As Carol paid for the coffees she looked back at her mother, still sitting in the iron café chair, still glancing now and then at the boy.

She passed the boy on her way to the pedestrian crossing. He stared at her, as so many boys did. She gave him a withering look and ran across the road. Her heart was pumping. The eyes that had stared at her were large and dark, dominating the face, unnervingly like her mother's.

Across the road she turned to look back. Above the massive granite block of the arts center the slender tower rose to a spire. Day and night birds circled around it. The boy was staring upward at them. She could see the whiteness of his throat, the slight bulge of his Adam's apple. There was a definite likeness to the woman sitting in the chair. They could be mother and son.

She shivered. Her mother used to be the sum and the boundary of her life, safe and dependable, not to be scrutinized or questioned, simply Mum, her mother. But the strange moods of the last year, the wild fantasies and irrational fears, and now this mad idea had turned her into a stranger. Carol realized she knew nothing about her mother, really, nothing about her past or her life—apart from the fact that she had left Carol's father when Carol was four years old. Her father had remarried, and had other children. Carol was on good terms with the whole family, but they lived on the other side of the continent in Perth and she saw them rarely.

The boy lowered his head, rubbed the back of his neck, turned, and saw Carol still standing on the opposite side of the road, staring. His face lit up and he smiled. He made a slight gesture with his hand as if he were going to wave. She didn't stop to see any more but ran to the park gate and through the gardens.

She runs past the lake, past some surprised ducks, through the herb garden, under the bamboo and the Moreton Bay figs, running because she's late, but not minding it, running also for the sheer joy of running, the sheer joy of being sixteen years old.

The day is bright after the rain, the gardens smell of fresh earth and flowers, the sky is miraculously not gray, but the palest of blues. Exotic birds screech in the greenery and swoop overhead, too swift to distinguish. And Carol runs, not exotic in her school uniform, not exotic at all, but inside she feels as swift and as careless as the birds.

"Carol, you've been told dozens of times!" Miss Walker stalked beside her to the school crossing. The English teacher had been waiting at the far gate to catch girls who walked to school through the Botanical Gardens. "It's for your own safety. Several very unsavory characters have been lurking by the gates, following girls to school, harassing them."

"I was late," Carol pleaded. "It's much quicker going through the gardens. And I was fine, wasn't I? I didn't see anyone. I'm not scared, anyway." She didn't want to listen to the teachers and their anxieties. She was afraid she would catch fear from them, and lose the freedom that fearlessness gave her. She despised the men who looked at her in the street, and felt that with her height, and her Doc Martens on her feet, no one would dare touch her or attack her..

"I'll let you off this time," Miss Walker said. "But you mustn't do it again. Otherwise you'll face some punishment."

Some punishment! What could they do to her? She nodded briefly to the teacher, and ran ahead up the stairs to her classroom.

At the end of the afternoon she tried to phone her father. It was usually a good time to catch him, since Perth was three hours behind Melbourne, but he was not in his office and there was no answer from his house. The phone rang and rang. In the end Carol gave up. She didn't know what she was going to tell him, what she wanted him to do, but she didn't want to be alone with her mother and not able to tell anyone.

She packed up her books, her mind in turmoil. Could

it be possible that the boy was her mother's child? Could he be her brother? But how come she had never heard of him before? No, she told herself, it was just another delusion. Her mother had seen a boy who looked enough like her to start weaving a story, who knew why? A hidden desire, maybe, the desire for more children, for boy children.

She walked back through the gardens after school, determined not to let anyone put fear into her, to catch her tram from outside the arts center. The boy was sitting on the parapet of the ornamental pond as if he was waiting for her. When he saw her he got up and wandered across the road. She just missed the tram. The next one would be in ten minutes. She didn't look at him, but she knew he was looking at her. He was approaching her, standing next to her. He would think she was interested in him because she had been staring at him. But she wasn't, not in that way, not at all. She tried to freeze him off, turn away from him, but she knew he was going to speak to her.

When he spoke, the words were unexpected and strange. She could hardly understand them.

"They ought to do something about the birds."

"What?"

"The birds. They keep circling the tower. They never rest. Even at night. They should take the spire down, turn the lights off at night. It's not fair on the birds to make them keep circling like that."

Carol looked up. The birds flew unceasingly around

the top of the spire. They looked like seagulls, or maybe pigeons. They were too high to see clearly.

"They'd fly away if they wanted to," she said. "Don't worry about them."

"But they don't," the boy replied. "They never fly away. They just keep circling and circling. There's something about the spire. They can't escape from it."

"Well, I don't know what to do," Carol snapped. "Phone the RSPCA or someone. Phone the city council."

"No one cares," the boy said sorrowfully.

The tram arrived with a rattle, and Carol got on. She didn't look at the boy again, but with sinking heart was aware that he had followed her. He sat down next to her.

"No one cares what happens to the birds, or the fish . . ." He fell silent for a moment as he thought about the fish.

"Oh God," Carol groaned to herself.

"The Murray's full of carp, you know. They're an introduced species, a pest."

He had been looking straight ahead, but now he turned and stared with glittering dark eyes at Carol. Just the way, she thought with foreboding, her mother looked at her, willing her to listen and believe. She couldn't stop herself looking back. The boy's sullen face lightened, and he smiled at her.

"At the Murray mouth, at Goolwa, the carp get swept out through the locks into the saltwater. They're freshwater fish, of course. You see them at the lock gates trying to swim back again. Eventually they die in the saltwater. Thousands of them. No one cares about them. There are too many of them.

Carol shuddered. There was something both pathetic and revolting about the image of the teeming, dying fish.

"Is that where you're from, Goolwa?" she said, trying to restore a note of normality into the conversation.

"I grew up there. My parents live there. But they're not my real parents. I was adopted. My real mother lives in Melbourne. That's why I'm here. I'm looking for her."

"This is my stop," she said hurriedly, though it wasn't. She'd have to walk for ages to get home. She leaped up and rang the bell.

"Will you meet me tomorrow?" he said, the dark eyes huge and tragic, just like her mother's.

"I can't, I'm sorry."

"I'll be at the arts center," he said, "if you change your mind."

Her mother was home, the house was clean, and delicious smells came from the kitchen. The dining room table was set with the good china, and candles stood in bottles, waiting to be lit.

So that's where the money went, Carol thought. "What's the celebration?" she said warily.

"I want us to have a special dinner together," her mother replied. "I've got something to tell you."

"Mum, I've got an awful lot of homework!"

"It's important, Carol."

Her mother seemed calm, but too controlled, as if she were holding something down. Her face, usually so pale, was flushed, and her eyes bright. She did not often drink, she distrusted alcohol, but she had bought a bottle of wine; now she drew the cork and poured herself a glass.

"Do you want some wine, Carol?"

"Okay." Carol often drank with her friends, but this was the first time she had shared wine with her mother. It made her feel different, grown up.

The food was wonderful, chicken risotto and green salad. Lately her mother had almost given up cooking, even though she had always been good at it. Carol ate hungrily. Her mother sipped a little wine, ate a mouthful of food, seemed about to speak, then took another mouthful.

"So what's so important?" Carol asked finally.

"There's something I've got to tell you. It's not easy. I've kept it secret for a long time. Even your father doesn't know."

"It's that boy, isn't it?" Carol said. "Is he really my brother?"

Her mother nodded. She looked at Carol with the dark eyes so like the boy's, and tears began to form in them.

"How old is he?" Carol said slowly. She felt a bit sick, either from the wine, or from shock, she wasn't sure.

"He's twenty years old today."

"It's his birthday?" Carol looked at the feast they had

shared. The ghost of the boy hovered momentarily at the table.

"I always try to make something special on his birthday," her mother said softly.

"You gave him up to be adopted?"

"I wasn't going to. I wanted to keep him. But then his father died . . ."

"Oh, Mum!"

The tears were pouring down her mother's cheeks now. Carol felt a rawness at the back of her throat, as if a sob were forming there. She swallowed hard, drank a mouthful of wine, and swallowed again.

"Does he know who you are? Have you talked to him?"

Her mother shook her head.

"Mum, are you sure about all this? How can you be certain if you haven't spoken to him?"

"I know," her mother said, placing her hand on her chest, the fingers between the collar bones. "A mother always knows."

"Are you going to tell him?"

"I want you to. And I've got something for you to show him."

"I'm not going to! I can't!"

Her mother rose from the table as if she hadn't heard Carol speak, and went into her bedroom. Carol could hear her pulling a suitcase out from under the bed. In a moment her mother returned with an old brown envelope. She placed it gently in front of Carol. "I want you to show this to him."

Carol picked up the envelope and studied it. It had a name and address on it, which had been inked out by someone, and an old stamp and postmark. She could just make out the date—22.12.75. "What is it?"

"Look inside."

Carol took a sheaf of papers out of the envelope— newspaper cuttings, letters, a birth certificate.

The first cutting she looked at was a picture of a crashed car. It was a total wreck, the metal twisted and smashed almost beyond recognition. *Local Man Killed in Horror Accident,* the caption read.

"This was . . . ."

"Shane Davies. My first love, I suppose you could say," her mother spoke from behind her hand. "I was six weeks pregnant. I hadn't even told him. He would have married me. He loved me."

The next cutting was also about the accident but was more of an obituary. There was a photo of a young man with a mop of dark curly hair, a crooked nose, and a wide grin. Shane Davies, twenty-one years old. A sports star, something of a hero to the small community in South Australia. A tragic loss.

Then there was a map of country South Australia, with an intersection on the road between Goolwa and Strathalbyn circled in red. A report of the inquest. A funeral notice. Everything looked so old and insignificant. It was hard to believe these few remains were evidence of the tragedy that had marked her mother's life.

"He . . . that boy grew up in Goolwa," Carol said. "He told me about the carp in the Murray."

"You spoke to him?"

"He sat next to me on the tram. He asked me to meet him again."

"Yes, you must. As soon as possible. You must give him the envelope. And tell him to come and see me. He must know who he is, where he comes from." Her mother spoke in short rapid gasps.

"He said he was looking for his real mother."

"I know. I had a phone call. That's how I knew who he was. I didn't want to see him at first. But I must. I must. He needs to know who he is and where he comes from. Everyone needs to know that."

Carol felt as if she was stifling. "It's nothing to do with me, Mum. It's your . . ." She was going to say problem, but that seemed too harsh. "Your business," she finished lamely. I shouldn't have to deal with this, she was thinking; it's not fair. I don't want a brother. I don't want to sort out something that happened all those years ago. I don't want to cope with this secondhand tragedy.

Her mother was weeping again, more noisily now. "I can't tell him. I can't. I can't face him yet. I want him to know the facts before I meet him. I want him to forgive me.

You've got to understand, Carol. I'll never be free until I've met him, until I've told him the truth. I've buried the truth for all these years. It's got to come out. Then I'll be free."

Carol is moved by these words. Though she hates catching other people's emotions, she is seduced into catching some of her mother's pain. The pain makes the past suddenly clear to her. The dark moments, the instability, the fears and fantasies all became understandable. Reluctantly she realizes she is part of this past and that she cannot cut herself off from it. She takes another mouthful of wine.

"All right, I'll go and meet him tomorrow."

She raced through the gardens at lunchtime, hoping to get there and back before afternoon school. All morning she had been rehearsing what she was going to say. *I know who your mother is. I am your half sister. My mother wanted you to see these things. They will tell you who your father was.*

The boy was there, watching the birds. The birds were still circling the spire. The boy's head turned as he watched them. Then he lowered his head and rubbed the back of his neck. He saw Carol and smiled his transforming smile. "Hello!" he said.

"Do you want to have a coffee?" she asked as neutrally as possible.

"Sure." He grinned at her and swaggered a little as they walked to a table.

Carol studied him as he went to order. He was slight like her mother, not like her at all. She was as tall as he, and more strongly built. He had their mother's dark coloring (although his father, Shane Davies, had had dark hair, too), whereas Carol was dark blond and blue-eyed like her father. No one would have ever picked them for brother and sister.

When he came back he sat down opposite her and stared at her. She took the envelope out of her bag and laid it on the table. "I'm only here," she said, "because my mother wanted me to come. She's the woman I was with yesterday."

He said nothing, just went on staring.

Carol plunged on. "You said you were looking for your mother . . ."

He nodded.

"Well, my mother, that woman, thinks she might be your mother."

He looked abruptly away, upward. "Is her name Marcia Wynton?"

"Yes."

"The name of the person I was told is my mother is Marcia Wynton. But they said she didn't want to see me."

"She does want to see you, but she's afraid."

He turned then and looked directly at her. "Why should *she* be afraid?"

"She thinks you may not forgive her."

The boy gave a short, astonished laugh and didn't say anything for a while. Then he said, "What's your name?"

"Carol."

"Carol Wynton?"

"Yes."

"I'm Steven Coggins. At least that's what my adopted parents called me. I hate Coggins. It's an ugly name. Wynton is much nicer." He fell silent again, then laughed in the same surprised way. "So you're my sister?"

"Half sister."

"Shame. I really fancied you."

Carol felt her face go hot, felt a flicker of something like fear. "Well, tough luck."

"Is your dad still around?"

"He married again. He's in Perth."

"Poor old Mum doesn't seem to have had much luck with men. I guess my dad walked out on her, too."

Carol found herself disliking him more and more. "My mother wants me to give you this," she indicated the envelope. "It's got a lot of stuff about your father in it." Then because that sounded so bald, she added, trying to sound gentle, "He died before you were born."

Steven was biting the nail of his right thumb. "You're very beautiful, you know. Is that why she kept you and gave me away?"

"She couldn't keep you," Carol said. "She was only

twenty herself. Your father was dead . . ."

He spoke as if he hadn't heard her. "Do you know what it was like? Can you imagine it? I never belonged anywhere. I was always the odd one out. I felt like the carp, struggling in the saltwater, trying to get back to the freshwater where I belonged. Dying in the saltwater."

He slid his hand into the envelope and drew out the pieces of paper.

"Christ!" he said when he saw the wrecked car. "What an idiot." He looked through the faded cuttings. "What are these supposed to mean?" he said in quiet anger. "This old junk is supposed to give me back my life?"

Carol jumped to her feet. "I've got to go, I've got to get back to school. Mum's going to be here tomorrow. If you still want to see her, you can meet her then."

Steven threw the cuttings down on the table and stood up. "I'll walk you back to school."

"No," she said. "I don't want you to." The wind was blowing the pieces of paper away. She scrabbled after them desperately, trying to retrieve the past. She shoved them back into the envelope and put it in her schoolbag.

Steven took her hand. "I'm your brother, I can walk with you." But the way he held it was not like a brother.

Carol wrenched her hand away from him and ran across the road. Without looking back she ran into the gardens. Steven ran after her. He was faster than she was and he caught up with her a few yards inside the gate.

"Don't run away from me, Carol. I just want to get to know you."

"I'm not sure I want to get to know you!"

"You liked me before. I saw you looking at me."

"I was only looking at you because my mother kept going on about you." She walked as swiftly as possible, striding out in her Doc Martens. He kept up with her.

"I'll carry your bag."

"No!" she said furiously, but he had already pulled it from her grasp. He held it out of her reach, laughing slightly. She wasn't going to have a struggle here with him over her bag. She gave in.

"Okay, but hurry up. I'm going to be late."

They passed the lake and the kiosk and began to climb the hill toward the far gate. Steven stopped alongside a stand of bamboo and looked back. Above the greenery, in the distance, the spire of the arts center could just be seen. Around it, looking no larger than flies, the birds kept circling.

"Come on!" Carol said.

He stood still. She went back to take her bag. Steven dropped it and grabbed her arms. "You're so beautiful," he said again. "I can't believe you. Just give me one kiss. Before anyone knows you're my sister. Now, while we've got this time. No one knows who we are."

"Let me go," she said, thinking *stay calm, stay calm, he won't hurt you* and then thinking *I don't know anything about him, I don't know who he is, maybe he's completely mad . . .*

He was holding her close to him, his leg pushed between hers. He was surprisingly strong. His hand was behind the back of her head, pushing her mouth toward his.

"Stop it," she screamed, no longer calm at all, just terribly angry. "Stop it!"

He stopped. "Okay!" he said. "It's no big deal."

"You bastard!"

"Hey, I wasn't going to rape you."

Carol picked up her school bag and walked away. Steven walked after her.

"Don't follow me!"

"Just making sure you get to school safely."

They could see the school buildings beyond the gate. Steven gave a low whistle. "Smart-looking school. Bit different from the area school I went to."

"I won a scholarship, if it's any of your business."

"Wow, bright as well as beautiful. You've got the lot, Carol." His mocking laughter followed her.

Carol stumbles to the gate, and it's almost a relief to be met by Miss Walker and to hear her shocked voice. "It's all right," she assures her. "I'm all right. No, it's not a stranger and he wasn't stalking or harassing or assaulting me. He's my brother, my brother, my brother."

And then the tears start to flow and pour on unchecked for her lost fearlessness, for her lost independence, for she knows she'll never be rid of him, or of her mother. They are her family. She is bound to them for life, bound by the invisible strands of love and fear and guilt and belonging.

And above the spire day and night still the birds keep circling.

A NOTE FROM GILLIAN RUBINSTEIN

I was born in England in 1942, during the Second World War. My parents divorced when I was about ten, and a few years later my mother and my stepfather went to live in Nigeria. I spent eight years flying out to Africa for holidays and going back to England to boarding school. I've always loved learning languages and I studied French and Spanish at Oxford University. I worked in the publishing industry and as a film critic and journalist before emigrating to Australia in 1973.

I started writing for children when my own children were in primary (elementary) school. My first novel, *Space Demons,* was published in 1986. Since then I've been a full-time writer and have eleven novels, several shorter books, and many short stories. I also work in youth theater, and have written eight plays. My most recent books published in America are *Galax-Arena* (1995) and *Foxspell* (1996). A fantasy adventure called *Under the Cat's Eye* will be published in the fall. My next projects are the screenplay for *Foxspell* and a sequel to *Galax-Arena.*

For the last fifteen years I've lived in Adelaide, South Australia, with my husband Philip, and our three children. I like reading, going to the cinema and theater, walking, swimming, gardening, and studying Japanese. I love animals and often write about my pets, at the moment a dog and three cats.

"And Still the Birds Keep Circling" began as the

germ of an idea when I was staying in Melbourne and noticed the birds that circle the spire of the arts center day and night. There was something unnerving and worrying about them. It was an image that returned strongly when I started thinking about a story on the theme "trapped." Like all my work, the story began with the characters—in this, Carol and her unstable mother. Carol thinks she is free from everything, and can do anything she wants, but family ties prove to be insidiously binding. Like the birds that circle the spire, and the carp that struggle to return to the freshwater, we all are ruled by deep instincts, needs, and fears that we only partly understand. I like exploring these feelings in my work.

Calvin felt weak and scared, but worst of all was the feeling of being totally alone. A voice screamed inside him to run, but in the next instant he felt something cold and hard ram his stomach. He looked down almost in wonder to see a small revolver jammed to his shirt. He looked up into the bigger boy's eyes and the cold blackness there made him think of the empty windows he'd seen. Slowly his hand went to his jeans and found his wallet.

MINIMUM WAGE

BY APOLLO

The last Greyhound bus was just like the first. Or the second, or the sixth. Calvin had lost count of how many he'd ridden in the past four days. Or had it been five? He couldn't remember ever being this tired in his life. That was funny because all he'd basically been doing was sitting on his butt, and for a sugarcane cutter, that should have been heaven.

He yawned and sat up in the seat, stretching his arms as he looked out the window to seemingly see the same sign he'd been seeing for days: GREYHOUND BUS DEPOT. The only difference was the smaller letters underneath: Oakland Welcomes You. Calvin read the words again, carefully, to make sure of the welcome part. He liked to read, even though his last teacher had told him he only read at the sixth-grade level. That was okay for comics, but the real world with all its signs and warnings got confusing when you couldn't read any better than that. But now, here in California, maybe he'd have the time to learn.

The bus came to a stop near the terminal door with a

last sigh of breaks. Calvin stood up a little stiffly and pulled his old nylon backpack from the overhead rack. People pushed roughly past. Calvin murmured excuse-me's, even though he was the one getting shoved. Walking to the front of the bus, he paused at the steps and turned to the driver.

"Thank you, suh. It was a nice trip."

The man behind the steering wheel was black. His eyes were hard at first, but then seemed to soften a bit after a second glance at Calvin. "You got people here, son?"

Calvin hesitated. He didn't like to lie, but . . . "Um, my uncle be comin' to meet me, suh."

The driver sighed as if he'd already heard all the lies in the world. "Y'all from Georgia, son?"

"Florida, suh."

The driver studied Calvin, his eyes with their cynical edge scanning the boy's panther-black body, which was clad in a tight white undershirt tank top and faded old 501 jeans. There wasn't an ounce of fat on Calvin's slim but rock-solid frame: small biceps bulged hard, and his sweat-dampened shirt clung to high jutting pecs and flat washboard stomach like a coat of paint. The driver's eyes lingered a moment on Calvin's face, handsome with a wide but small-bridged nose and expressive full lips, yet looking younger than his thirteen years because of big long-lashed ebony eyes beneath an Afro puff of soot-colored hair. Finally the man looked at Calvin's hands, strong and sinewed but scarred with old cuts.

The driver sighed again. "This ain't the cane-brake, son. An' it sure as hell ain't the Green Pastures. Y'all watch yourself, hear me?"

"Um . . . yes, suh."

It was good of the driver to warn him, thought Calvin as he got off the bus and walked into the station. But he wasn't just a fool kid who'd run away: Fact was there'd been nothing to run away from. He'd been alone since his father had passed two years before. Life in cane country had been hard, and he'd done a man's work for years. And like a man he'd demanded and gotten a man's pay from his fat Cuban boss. But life had to be more than just slaving for minimum wage.

He looked around the busy waiting room. Everyone in the North seemed to be in some kind of big hurry all the time. If they weren't actually rushing from place to place they were fidgeting where they stood as if they had ants in their pants. He supposed that was normal for northern white folks, but all the black people here were doing it, too. He saw many different shades and shapes of black faces, but just like the white, brown, and Asian ones, none looked very friendly. Two boys stood by a Coke machine, one in a puff coat and beanie even though it was July, the other in T-shirt and jeans. They were about his own age, but cool city Brothers and gave him brief smirks when they noticed his hair and battered old Nikes. He saw a pretty girl and felt her eyes run over his body. He'd never given much thought to how he looked . . . yeah, he had muscles but they came from swinging a machete or stacking cane in the sweltering sun. The girl gave him the ghost of a smile, and he felt better for that, but then she left with her parents. About to move on, he noticed a white man smiling in his direction. The man wore pilot-style sunglasses, so Calvin couldn't see his eyes, but since the smile looked so friendly, Calvin figured it was for someone behind him. Then he saw a big black security guard giving him the glare that meant he would either have to show his bus ticket or get his ass out. His ticket was all used up, so he headed for the front doors.

He passed the station restaurant, and sudden hunger cramped his stomach. He had eaten almost nothing in the last few days, but since he didn't have much money he'd thought it was better to save it. In a city you just didn't unroll a blanket and sleep under the stars. He would have to find a place to stay tonight, wash the traveling dust from his body, and then search for some work in the morning. There had to be construction going on, and he could swing a pick or shovel dirt as well as any man. He was young, strong, and willing to learn; someone would want him for something.

Out on the sidewalk he paused, wondering which way to go. A trio of shabby taxis were lined up at the curb and their drivers, all black, were leaning against one talking and reading a paper. "Um?" asked Calvin, "Do y'all know where there be a good roomin' house?"

The drivers glanced at him and exchanged smirks. One pointed. "Try the Parc Towers, boy."

Calvin looked to where a pair of huge new skyscrapers loomed blocks away, all glass and shiny steel. He turned from the men, his face flushing as they busted into laughter. Tugging at his pack straps, he trudged down the sidewalk toward what was obviously the poorer section of town. To hell with those fools, he'd find a good place on his own! He began to picture it in his mind as he walked: a small clean room, maybe with its own sink. There was a book in his pack that he'd bought in New Orleans. It was the first real book he'd ever owned, and he wanted to try reading it all the way through. Its title was *Invisible Man*, and it seemed to be about poor black kids back in the days when life was really hard.

Calvin walked on, half lost in his thoughts of the new life he would build for himself. Part of that life would be the freedom to relax if he wanted to. There was nothing wrong with work, but too much of it trapped you. It was late afternoon and the sidewalk was baking under the sun, though the heat was nothing compared to Florida. The people he saw were mostly black, with a few who looked Cuban but were probably something else, and an occasional Asian. Calvin said hi to them at first: Some replied but seemed uneasy or suspicious; all acted slightly surprised. After a while he stopped greeting them. There were kids, too, black and brown, some on bikes or skateboards.

All looked well fed, some even fat. That was a good sign, Calvin thought; fat was a luxury and he wouldn't have minded a little to pad his own solid contours.

After a couple of blocks the sidewalks got rough and cracked, and his old Nikes crunched through bottle glass. The street was lined with buildings of brick, concrete, and stucco. Many were old and run-down, a few abandoned with broken or boarded-up windows. On a corner ahead he saw a grimy old four-story building with a faded sign that said Hotel. It looked like a place he could afford until he could get a job and find something better. But when he reached the front entrance he saw that the doors were nailed shut. The entryway walls were covered with spray-painted symbols and words, and the sour reek of wine and beer and piss wrinkled his nose. Calvin sighed and went back out onto the sidewalk. He stared up at one of the broken windows and into deep blackness. Strangely, that empty blackness made him sad.

"Hey, bro!"

Calvin turned to see a boy about his age, in baggy jeans and hoodie. "Wanna buy some weed, man?"

Calvin felt uneasy. "Um . . . no, thanks."

The other boy scowled and strutted away. "Square-ass little mark!" he spat over his shoulder.

Calvin began walking again, passing more ancient buildings, some apartment projects, and a few shabby houses where old people sat on crumbling porches, and near-naked kids played with big water guns in weedy yards. Further on he saw storage lots piled with junk cars and scrap metal and guarded by dogs of no real breed who snarled and bared razor teeth through rusty chain-link fences. Nothing in this place looked friendly or hopeful, and Calvin began to wonder if he'd gone too far. This was the same kind of setting he'd seen from the buses passing through other cities, and wasn't what he'd traveled thousands of miles to find. He turned around and began walking back toward the big new buildings that towered in the distance.

The sun had almost set when Calvin came to a small corner liquor store. His stomach ached and rumbled, and he felt a little dizzy. That was strange, he thought; working twelve hours in the blazing sun had never made him feel this tired. Going into the store, he bought a sandwich and a Coke from the Asian man at the counter. Back outside, he leaned against the wall and ate. The sandwich was soggy and small, something that might have been chicken, but he wolfed it down with gulps of soda and wanted another. But more food would have to wait: Streetlights were coming on as night set in, and he still had no place to sleep.

Another street seemed to lead straighter toward the city's better section, and he took it and hurried along as the shadows grew darker around him. He started to feel twinges of fear and they got harder and harder to fight. Maybe it was because he began to realize that he had to keep moving in a city, that there was no place where he could lie down and rest.

He felt a little better when he saw that the neighborhood seemed to be improving; the houses a bit more well kept, though most still had bars on their windows. The sky above the streetlamps was almost black now. There were no more young children, except for a group of boys no older than eight who clustered on a corner and smoked cigarettes. They watched Calvin hurry past, and their eyes reminded him of the junkyard dogs . . . to show them any fear would bring an attack. He saw few adults as night deepened. Then he noticed another boy about seventeen waking toward him. The kid was broad-chested and wore a Raiders jersey, big jeans, and a black baseball cap twisted sideways. A huge gold herringbone chain encircled his neck. Even though Calvin moved aside, the big boy slammed a shoulder into his chest, then turned with a scowl.

"The fuck you walk into my goddamn shoulder for, nigga?"

Calvin was trying to get his breath back. ". . . I sorry, brutha . . . I . . ."

"Shut the fuck up!" the kid hissed. He checked to make sure the street was clear. "Gimme your wallet, an' maybe I won't leave your fuckin' brains all over my sidewalk!"

Calvin felt weak and scared, but worst of all was the feeling of being totally alone. A voice screamed inside him to run, but in the next instant he felt something cold and hard ram his stomach. He looked down almost in wonder to see a small revolver jammed to his shirt. He looked up into the bigger boy's eyes, and the cold blackness there made him think of the empty window he'd seen. Slowly his hand went to his jeans and found his wallet. The big boy snatched it and spat.

"Thanks . . . *brother*." He turned casually and walked off down the street as if nothing at all happened.

For a minute or so Calvin only stood there. It had happened so *fast!* It was nothing like he'd seen in the movies . . . those scenes where he'd pictured himself as a comic book hero fighting off his attackers. A boy had just walked up to him, shoved a gun to his stomach, and then walked away. Now he had no money, no place to sleep, and nobody cared. As if in a daze he walked on. Streetlamps flickered with a lonely glow, and cars cruised by going somewhere while Calvin was headed nowhere. He walked, turning corners with no sense of direction. The people he passed might have been ghosts for all they meant to him. His body felt numb. Vaguely he realized he was near the Greyhound station again, in front of the abandoned hotel. He stood for a few minutes, staring up at black windows that seemed to grin down like eye sockets in a skull. The air had grown cold, and he shivered. He thought of the warm bus station, but knew they would just run him out if he tried to go back there. Finally he crept into the shadow-haunted, piss-smelling entryway and pulled a ragged gray Tampa Bay sweatshirt from his pack and put it on. Then he sank down, huddling into the darkest corner. He buried his face against his updrawn knees. Tears filled his eyes, and he cried.

Cars passed by on the street, their headlights seeming to leave things even darker when they were gone. Then, dimly through his sobbing, he heard a car pull up to the curb. It was probably a cop, but he was too tired to run. Besides, they would probably shoot him if he did. At least there were beds in prison. He barely lifted his head as the car door opened and footsteps came toward him. All he could see at first were shoes. Then he realized that they were those kind of leather sneakers that rich people wore to go boating. He did look up then, seeing a white man dressed in khaki slacks and a light blue button-front shirt under an open safari jacket. He scented soap, aftershave, and expensive cigarettes. Was this a plainclothes cop? He raised his eyes further to see the same man who had smiled at him in the bus station. He looked to be in his early thirties, with longish hair the color of sand and a small mustache that matched it. The man was smiling again, without his sunglasses now, and Calvin could see that the smile was for him. Right then any expression that wasn't of hate or disgust would have melted Calvin's heart. And any voice not a curse or a threat could have ruled him. The man smiled, and his voice was kind.

"Are you all right, son?"

For a second Calvin almost burst into tears again. But he made himself get to his feet and tried to keep his chin from quivering, while pretending to wipe something from his eye. "Um . . . sho, mister. I be okay."

Any fool could have seen that he wasn't okay, but the man seemed to know that Calvin needed pride. He didn't seem shocked that a boy was huddling in a doorway at night, but he did seem concerned.

"I know how it is on the mean streets, son. You're hungry and cold and nobody cares. You might even be a little afraid."

Calvin stood a little straighter. "Well . . . I is kinda hungry, suh. See, I got robbed tonight. All my money. I was gonna get me a hotel room . . . find me a job in the mornin'."

The man nodded as if he'd heard many such stories but, unlike the bus driver, he seemed to know Calvin was telling the truth. And the man seemed to respect him . . . he wasn't just another dirty, lying nigger but a real person with feelings.

"You just got into town, right, son?"

Seeing Calvin hesitate, the man smiled again. "I saw you at the Greyhound station. You were wearing a tank top then."

Calvin glanced down at his sweatshirt. "Yeah. Don't got many clothes. Don't even got a jacket, matter-of-fact. See, the weather be warmer where I come from."

The man nodded. "I thought you must have come from somewhere else. The South, maybe? Mississippi, Louisiana?"

"Florida, suh. I used to work in the cane fields."

"That's what I would have guessed next. I could see by your build that you've worked hard. Only real work gives a young man muscles like you have . . . chest like bricks, those fine strong arms."

Calvin straightened his back even more and expanded his chest a little. The man's words warmed him, and they were only the honest truth. "Yes, suh. I be strong. I be a good worker." He hesitated again, then asked, "Um, y'all wouldn't be knowin' where I could find me some work, suh?"

The man seemed to consider. "Hmmm, I just might." But then he looked faintly troubled. "Mind if I ask how old you are?"

Calvin's heart sank. This was just what he'd been afraid of . . . that some stupid law would keep him from getting a job. It was funny that kids could be allowed to starve, but not to work. "Um . . . sixteen, suh," he finally said, hating himself.

The man's smile showed that he understood, and Calvin felt better. The man glanced down the empty street before looking at Calvin again. "The truth is, son, it's not so much your age, but this job takes a lot of muscle."

Calvin held out his arm and flexed it. "Feel that, suh!"

The man gave Calvin's bicep a gentle squeeze. "Well, I've seen your arms and they look strong enough."

The man's tone was kind, but Calvin heard doubt in it, too. His chance was slipping away! Desperately he stripped off his sweatshirt and then peeled off his tank top. He thrust out his chest and tried to stand proud. "See me, suh! I strong as a ox!"

The man's touch was gentle on Calvin's chest, his fingertip tracing the muscles. Again he seemed to consider, stepping back a pace and regarding Calvin's half-naked body while fingering his chin in thought. Calvin held his breath, hoping against hope. Finally the man smiled again. "You remind me more of a young panther." He held out a pale hand. "I'll give you a try, son. My name's Tony."

"Calvin, suh." Letting out a sigh of relief, Calvin took the man's soft hand. They shook like equals. Then Tony picked up Calvin's things. "I've got a spare room at my house. You can stay there tonight." Then he paused. "If you'd like to?"

It seemed a silly question to ask a boy who was obviously homeless, but then this kind white man understood dignity. "Yes, suh. I wouldn't mind."

Tony chuckled and put a hand on Calvin's shoulder. "I don't suppose you'd mind a little dinner, either?"

It was a joke, and Calvin laughed to show he knew it. He reached for his tank top, but Tony just smiled. "No offense, son, but these things could do with a washing. The car's plenty warm . . . unless you're shy?"

"No suh. Not a bit shy." Calvin spent half his life shirtless, though it did feel a bit strange to be getting into a shiny red Mercedes at night in only his jeans and Nikes. But the soft leather seat felt good to his skin. Tony got in, and the car purred away. Hip-hop music bumped low from powerful speakers. Calvin gazed out: It was hard to believe that only minutes before he'd been shivering in those streets and not knowing what more he could do. Now he was in an expensive and beautiful car, and the future seemed suddenly bright!

"Don't suppose you're a drinking man, Calvin?" asked Tony.

"Um, now an' then, suh."

"Just call me Tony." He swung the car into a liquor store parking lot and returned a few minutes later with a forty-ounce of Olde English. "Take firsts," he said, offering it.

Calvin twisted off the cap. The truth was he'd only had a few beers in his life, but the ice-cold malt tasted so fine sliding down his dry throat. He passed the bottle to Tony and suddenly laughed.

"What's funny, Calvin?"

"I was just thinkin'; if I right now seen that nigger who rob me, I axe you to stop so's I could go shake his hand!"

A few more swigs of malt on his near-empty stomach

and Calvin was feeling free as a bird. That feeling increased when he saw they were leaving the city behind and climbing up into what seemed to be foothills. He relaxed back in the soft leather and sighed. Nothing in life was really free: His father had told him that many times. He would probably have to work his ass off tomorrow, but at least there wouldn't be cane to cut in California.

They had entered a rich-looking neighborhood up in the hills. Calvin looked down and saw what might have been the whole city of Oakland spread out below. Tony pulled the Mercedes into a driveway and cut the engine. "Well, here we are, Panther-boy."

Calvin got out of the car and stood for a moment. The night air up here was chill, but he could hardly feel it with most of a forty inside him. The house was small, but looked expensive as hell. It was painted white and boasted a pretty green lawn like the perfect ones Calvin had seen in movies. There were trees and shrubs and a gurgling fountain. Calvin wondered if the job Tony had in mind was something as simple as doing yard work? But who needed muscles to mow a lawn? "Um?" he asked. "Is the back yard bigger?"

"A little," said Tony. "And there's a pool. You like to swim?"

Calvin laughed. "Sho. Long's there ain't no 'gators I got to share the water with!" He was a little unsteady on his feet as he followed Tony, who carried his pack and shirts, up the steps and into the house. They walked down a short hall-way and into a small living room. There was a couch, a TV, and a glass coffee table with magazines scattered on top that seemed to be mostly about art and photography to Calvin's casual glance. The next room was a kitchen and dining room combination. Tony stopped. "This may be about as far as you want to go tonight."

"Huh?" asked Calvin, finding that he was a little bit drunk and slightly confused.

"You *are* still hungry, aren't you?"

Calvin laughed. "Oh, Yeah. Got that right!"

"Good. I'll put on some steaks. Bathroom's just down the hall there, and your bedroom's the one on the left. You have plenty of time for a shower, if you want."

Calvin glanced down at himself. "'Spect I could use one."

Tony gave Calvin his things. "You'll find some pajamas in the bedroom drawer. They're my nephew's, and you're about the same size. You can wear them if you like. We'll wash your clothes in the morning."

"Sho, Tony." Calvin turned to go, but Tony spoke. "Say cheese."

"Huh?" Calvin turned around just in time to be blinded by a camera flash. He blinked, then frowned. "Um, don't take this wrong, Tony, but I seen some things on TV about stuff like what you just done. I mean, takin' kids' pitchers naked."

Tony laughed and handed Calvin a Polaroid. "Are you naked?"

"Um, well, no."

"The picture's yours, Calvin. Tear it up if you want. I just thought you'd like it. See what I mean about you looking like a wild young panther?"

Calvin felt more like a fool than a panther for saying those things as he watched the first picture of himself he'd ever had develop right in his own hand like magic.

Tony's voice took on a slightly hurt tone. "There's a lock on the bathroom door, Calvin. And the bedroom door, too."

Calvin felt stupid. "I sorry, Tony. I think I be just a little bit drunk, is all."

Tony smiled again. "Aw, go on and shower, Panther-boy."

The hot shower felt so good, it was almost like a sin, and Calvin would have felt like an ungrateful shithead if he'd locked the door. With a big fluffy towel around his waist he went into the bedroom . . . *his* bedroom, at least for tonight. It seemed like a movie star's room, thick white carpet, the biggest bed he'd ever seen, a TV, stereo, and stuff he recognized from TV commercials as being a Sony Play-Station. Some sort of contraption that looked like a weight-training bench stood by curtained sliding-glass doors. Calvin parted the curtain and peeped out, seeing a patio and small swimming pool. Tony's nephew had to be the luckiest boy in the world! Leaving his pack and clothes on a chair, he opened the dresser drawer to find the pajamas Tony had told him about. There were several pairs and they seemed to be silk. One pair was midnight black, another gold and spotted like leopard skin, another orange and striped like a tiger. He chose the last, plain white. They were something like karate clothes, with no buttons on the shirt, and seemed to be made for a boy just his size. They felt good on his freshly showered body. Another wonderful thing was the smell of broiled steak in the air. His mouth watered as he padded up the hall, and his stomach growled like a hungry lion.

"You look great, Panther-boy," said Tony as Calvin came into the kitchen. He pointed to the table where the meal waited, a huge slab of meat on one plate, a smaller one on the other. "The panther-sized one's yours. Like some more malt to go with it?"

"Sho!" said Calvin, sitting down and digging in.

A little while later, full of food and malt, Calvin sprawled back in his chair and patted his now drum-tight stomach. "I could get fat real easy livin' this kinda life," he said, and chuckled.

Tony, who sat across the table from him smoking a thin brown cigarette, frowned slightly. "That's something you can't do, I'm afraid."

"Well, I s'pose if that work be as hard as you make it sound, I don't need to worry."

Tony smiled again. "Oh, it's hard all right." He waved a hand toward the big refrigerator. "You can eat as much as you want, drink as much as you want, but you start getting fat and flabby and you're out of a job. There's a Soloflex in your room, and *part* of your job is using it every day to keep that body of yours looking just like that picture I gave you."

"Well, what *is* my job, Tony? . . . Um, an' don't take this wrong, but I got to get 'least minimum wage."

Tony laughed. "You'll find out in the morning. And I guarantee you'll do a lot better than minimum wage." He glanced at his Rolex. "A strong young man needs his sleep to stay that way." He rose. "We've got a long day tomorrow. Sweet dreams, Panther-boy."

A little bit drunk and slightly confused once more, Calvin went down the hall to his room. He was asleep the second his head hit the pillow. His dreams were beautiful and free.

He woke to find early morning sunlight sifting in through the curtains. The bedside clock read five-thirty, and the house was quiet. He sat up and looked around the room, hardly daring to believe that this wasn't a dream and he was really going to wake up in the abandoned hotel's piss-slimed entrance. He slipped from the bed to peer through the curtains. The backyard was surrounded by a high brick wall. There was green lawn, and the sun's sparkle made the pool's turquoise water look tantalizing. In another dresser drawer he found silk bikini briefs in animal patterns like the pajamas. Grinning, he pulled on a leopard-skin pair, then paused to study himself in the mirror. "Whattup, Panther-boy?" he asked his reflection.

The water was wonderful, and he swam for almost an hour. Life could be beautiful with the freedom to do what you wanted. The sun was warm, and he climbed out to sit at the end of the diving board and dangle his toes in the water. Then he turned as Tony came out through the sliding doors in a terry cloth robe with two tall glasses of what looked like orange juice.

"Yo, Panther-boy, like a mimosa?"

Calvin padded over and took a glass. He sipped. "Mmm! That's good, Tony."

Tony sat down in a plastic pool chair. "Orange juice and champagne. Best way to start the day. You looked great sitting there on the board all shiny and wet. I'd like take some pictures of you like that . . . if you aren't shy about it."

Calvin was sitting on the tile at Tony's feet. The sun seemed to caress his ebony skin, and the mimosa tasted extra fine. "I ain't shy, Tony. Just like you been tellin' me, I be handsome an' strong. Why I want to be shy over it?"

Tony smiled. "I bet you get lots of girls with that body."

Now Calvin did feel shy. "Well, um truth is I just never had much time. An' girls is kinda hard to talk to."

Tony laughed. "That's the truth!"

Calvin drained his glass. "Um, so what be my job, Tony? Look like that there hedge could use trimmin'."

"There's a Jap comes in once a week to do the yard." Tony seemed to think for a minute. When he spoke again, his voice was serious. "You think you'd like living here, Calvin? Being the Panther-boy? All this is yours to use . . . the pool, your own room, this house and all the things in it?"

Calvin felt confused again, slightly buzzed from the drink. "But . . . what I got do, Tony?"

Tony shrugged. "Keep in shape. Swim. Use the weights. Hell, trim the hedge if it makes you happy . . ." Tony's voice trailed off. Then he added softly, "You'd be meeting some of my friends from time to time. Mostly here, occasionally at a hotel down in Oakland or over in San Francisco. They like handsome young men like you."

A chill ran down Calvin's spine. He wasn't that big of a fool not to know what Tony wanted him for! He sprang to his feet, feeling suddenly naked despite the briefs. "Hell, no, mister! I be nobody's ho! I gettin' out of here right now!"

Tony didn't seem surprised or angry. He just sipped his mimosa and smiled. "Well, that's your choice, Calvin." He chuckled. "I'm not a slaver. I'm offering everything I told you about. By the way, your wages would have been a hundred dollars an hour, when you're working. Slightly above 'minimum,' wouldn't you say? And I care about my boys;

they don't get hurt." He took another sip of his drink. "With your body and face there could be a good chunk of change in pictures, too. Not to mention films. A lot of my friends are in the movie business." Then he sighed and leaned back in the chair. "But your old clothes are in there on the bed. Sorry I can't give you a ride back to your hotel. And I'd get out of this neighborhood as fast as possible if I were a young black male."

It was strange that Calvin was suddenly more scared than angry as he went to the sliding doors. There was his ragged backpack, dirty jeans, and tank top on the bed, his worn-out Nikes on the floor: all that he owned in the world. Where would he go from here? He looked around the beautiful room. Tony was just gazing at the pool's sparkling water, his back turned.

"Um, so what happened to the other boy who was here before me?"

Tony didn't turn around. "He let himself get fat and lazy, and lost his job. Maybe he took his money and went back home. Nobody damaged him, if that's what you're thinking."

"Was he the Panther-boy, too?"

Tony turned around. "You're the only one, Calvin. I've never seen a boy as handsome as you. You're special to me."

It was funny how those stupid words from a pimp could sound so kind and good.

A NOTE FROM APOLLO

I was born in Oakland in 1980, and have lived in various areas of that city all my life. At the age of twelve, I started writing stories reflecting inner-city life. I had my first story published in *Zyzzyva* magazine at age thirteen. Soon after, I put together a collection of short stories entitled *Concrete Candy*, published by Anchor-Doubleday.

Concrete Candy consists of six stories that deal with kids living the violent and tragic life of the inner city and how they survive. The stories are a gritty portrayal of life on the street, but are mixed with elements of fantasy and magic realism.

Concrete Candy was released in April 1996 and has also been published in Denmark and France.

I have spoken at Stanford University, as well as various junior high and high schools throughout California. I have also spoken at California Youth Authority, hoping to uplift kids and show them there are ways out of their self destructive lifestyle.

My book, *The Fence*, is now looking for publication. It is a futuristic novel in which black ghettos all across America have been shut off from the rest of the city by huge fences, similar to the situation in the Warsaw ghettos in Poland during Hitler's reign. The story is a satire on America's obsession to solve the "gang and drug" problems of the inner city, and rings reminiscent of George Orwell's classic, *1984*.

I hope to steer kids away from gang violence with my stories and talks.